WITH A VENGEANCE

By

D. J. ADAMSON

Horatio Press

Mystery • Science Fiction • Suspense

First Printing 2023

ALSO BY THE AUTHOR

TO KATHY JEAN,
WHO HAS ALWAYS KNOWN SHE HAS CHOICES.

Now.

I want it now!

If later, would it be as sweet?

Can truth be untainted by time,

Aged, but knowing, witnessed, healed?

No, seek now.

Fresh from the womb of hurt.

Take on life, not as it comes, but with a vengeance

While sand seeps through fingers

And breath depletes.

--Lillian Dove

Doing it differently,

But where does truth lie?

In the past or the present?

In the first or the second feeling or thought?

Moved by emotion or justified?

The past opens the future, and the future

Becomes bygone, only to renew once more.

--Lillian Dove

Contents

CHAPTER ONE
SUNDAY, FEBRUARY 8TH

"Lillian!"

"Lillian Dove, wake up!"

I opened an eye and saw Dahlia standing over me. "What time is it?"

"Eight o'clock." She was wearing a new two-in-one teal sweater cardigan. The color of the cardigan emphasized the blue in her eyes and fired up her recently dyed red hair.

"It's Sunday," I returned. "I have at least another hour to sleep. Go away." Every nerve in my body told me to ignore her. I buried deeper beneath the covers.

Dahlia shook me again. "I need you to get up."

I shuddered a strangled sigh. "What for? What's wrong?"

"Nelly called. You need to take me to Oaks. Mrs. Goyen is sick, and she won't make it another day."

I half sat up, confused. "I don't remember a friend named Goyen."

"She's not a friend. She hates my guts. Now, get up."

I shut my eyes and laid back down. Pulled the comforter over my head. She pulled the comforter off. "Lillian!"

I opened one eye. Opening both would have told her she was getting to me. "Why would she ask for you if she hates your guts?"

"That's for me to know and none of your business. Now, come on." She grabbed my arm and tugged.

I sighed. "You're not going to let me go back to sleep, are you?"

"Does it look like I am going to?"

Demanding for me to do something I didn't want to do wasn't new—like I was a child, and she was my mother. Well, she is my mother. But I call her Dahlia. I had a childhood history of her waking me up to help care for my father. I have a low, sweet cozy childhood memory limit. But I've let my Dahlia resentments go. Not because I aim for sainthood. But because the past is just too damn heavy to carry around.

"Fine," I acquiesced. "Let me get dressed."

"Hurry," she urged. Always getting in the last word.

I yanked myself out of bed. I got dressed in jeans and a t-shirt I had made for a store advertisement for my Triple A Discount Liquor store. The t-shirt read: GO AHEAD, DARE TO DISCOUNT ME. Located in Frytown, Iowa, the store is known by locals as having the best prices this side of Walmart.

When I entered the living room, I found Dahlia on the couch with her coat on. My cat Bacardi lay next to her. Scrunched face, his yellow-ish-brown fur fizzed out from his body as if he'd stuck his claw in a light socket. He is my cat, but he had taken a liking to Dalhia after she moved in.

Bacardi looked at me cross-eyed, stood, arched his back, and hissed.

"Have you fed him yet?" I asked Dahlia.

"Would I leave without giving him his breakfast?" she replied with a smirk.

I thought I relocated from Davenport, Iowa, to Frytown to care for Dahlia. My brother Frank implied she didn't have long to live. For which, at first, I was grateful. But now, I hoped there was still time for us to have a normal relationship.

Then again, maybe hope is a figment of my imagination. Or an illusion like a wish taken before blowing out all the candles on a birthday cake. In thinking about it, maybe I have too many candles and not enough breath.

Plus, this wasn't how I planned to start my day. I wanted to sleep in. Then lay and contemplate my life. Access where I was going and how to get there faster. I no longer wanted to live on a whim, but live life with a vengeance. Take on a day, NOT let the day take me on.

"Let's go then," I said, making this my choice, not Dahlia's. And to show my breath of reason, I added, "I need to do a couple of things before opening the store, anyway."

Dahlia struggled off the couch, arthritic knees giving her trouble this morning.

I would have gone to help her, but Dahlia is a proud, independent woman. She wasn't ready to be old yet.

"Yep, let's get going," she rasped. "I need to get there before it's too late."

I looped my purse over my shoulder. Opened the door. Inhaled a deep breath, still a bit worried about how the day wasn't starting the way I'd planned and wondering how to get it back under my control.

Convalescent hospitals have a distinct atmosphere. They radiate a blended scent of sterilizing alcohol, urine, and unwashed bodies. And this morning, an essence of gruel. Sounds echoed off the walls. Knocks on doors. Good mornings exchanged. Bedpans clanging.

"Good morning, Lillian. Dahlia," Nelly called from the reception desk.

Dahlia grunted hello and thumped her walker straight down a corridor. I checked in with Nelly to learn what she knew about the urgency of Dahlia's visit.

This morning, Nelly Crow wore a white nurse's smock with angel imprints over a long blue cotton skirt. Nelly Crow covered her hair with a white Mennonite cap while wearing a white nurse's smock with angel imprints over a long blue cotton skirt..

I said, "I'm sorry to hear about Mrs. Goyen."

"Poor thing," she replied sorrowfully. "She hasn't been the same since Mr. Goyen passed."

"Dahlia said she doesn't have long to live."

Alarmed, Nelly squeaked, befuddled. "I hope she didn't go into Mrs. Goyen's room with that attitude. Mrs. Goyen is having respiratory problems and recovering from a cold. But she's going to be fine." Nelly checked out the corridor where Dahlia had disappeared. She seemed unsure whether she should stay at the station or go check to make sure Dahlia wasn't making a list of Mrs. Goyen's funeral arrangements.

She reasoned, "I may have told Mrs. Dove it would be good to come down to see Mrs. Goyen today before it got too late. But I meant late in the day. I said nothing about dying. And I didn't think you'd bring your mother down this morning. Aren't you opening the store today?"

"It's Sunday," I reminded her.

"Oh, that's right. You open later on Sundays."

She sucked her bottom lip. Continued to gaze in the direction Dahlia had gone.

I offered, "Dahlia must have misunderstood. You know how she can be." I smiled and winked.

Nelly attempted a returned smile.

When Dahlia lived at Oaks Manor, she established a reputation for being difficult. I thought it best to leave before causing Nelly to worry any further. "Look, I have a couple of errands to run. I'll be back to get Dahlia in an hour."

Nelly made a mewing sound. She glanced at her watch.

"I'll try to be quick."

CHAPTER TWO

"Look what the cat dragged in!" Donna Stockman twirled around in her ergonomic chair and beamed a radiant smile. Then she pointed at the T-shirt I was wearing and busted out laughing. "Who would ever dare to discount you?"

I'd made some good friends when working for the Frytown Police Department. And Donna remained number one in my book. She's like a dark, chocolate-dipped cherry, a little bitter on the outside, but once you get to know her, sweet and gooey inside.

I stopped at the station to ask her for dinner on Friday night. Saturday was Valentine's Day and her birthday.

Donna was wearing a blue shirt, untucked, with FPD, *We Serve Our Community*, stitched on the front. She sat grinning like a cat that had eaten the canary and could see another bird ready to escape out of the cage. She step-rolled her chair over to where she kept her own personal Mr. Coffee. "Want a cup?"

I waved off the offer. "I can't stay but a minute."

She picked up a pint jar half full of something dark, swirling in some juice.

"Anything going on?" I asked.

She shrugged. "Some guy got so hammered he fell walking his bike. I sent Sergeant Miner to help him wheel it home to sleep it off. Then, not a moment later, I sent Garth to Rooster Creek to arrest some sauced hen. Spring is coming, girly."

She fingered something out of the jar with her long, red, manicured nails. Counting, "One, two...when I first got in, Will Walton called and said Sam Roe's cows were over at his place. Claimed one moo-ved up onto his front porch." She chuckled at her joke. "Moo-ved up," puckering her lips with the moooo. "He warned me if we didn't get there fast, he would get out his shotgun and pack his freezer full of beef. Three...four."

"Fairly normal morning, then?"

"Yep. Pretty boring." She popped what she'd fingered out of the jar into her mouth and smacked her lips.

"What do you have there?" I nodded to the jar.

"It's my new diet. Eat four of these raisins every hour, and they guarantee you'll lose ten pounds."

"Who guarantees?"

She nestled herself in her chair. Her eyebrows moved to an uneven position. One eye stayed below her vintage glasses, while the other rose—clearly puzzled.

A grin stretched across her lips. "Who cares who? It's working. I've got a lot more energy. And I've lost three pounds."

Donna considered even a pound a notable amount to lose. She was what some call large-boned.

"What's that the raisins are soaking in?"

"Vodka."

"Vodka?"

"Yep. They say it's good for arthritis, too." She smiled big.

"Donna." I giggled. "Raisins soaked in vodka sounds a lot like jello shots. You feel good because you're getting a buzz."

This time, both eyebrows arched, sending her glasses to slip to the middle of her nose. "I don't think," she squinted her eyes at me, "a handful of raisins is going to get me buzzed."

"A handful? I thought you said four every hour."

"Well, hon, if I set my clock and woke up every hour, I wouldn't be able to get out of bed in the morning. So, I take a big handful right before bed." She smiled and stretched her arms above her head, emitting a loud yawn. "Been sleeping like a baby."

"I bet." I wondered how often her fingers had dipped into the jar this morning.

"Hey," Donna exclaimed. "Since the phone lines are quiet, would you mind taking over while I go to the restroom? I like this diet, but it's cleaning me out."

Hence, I thought, the pounds she'd lost.

I'd never handled the dispatch lines. The FPD had three dispatchers. It's their job to respond to emergency or non-emergency calls. They send the officers out on calls and inform them of the code they're facing once they get there.

"I don't know, Donna. You know I don't have the experience or the certification to..."

"Oops," she jumped out of her chair. "Just for a minute. Don't worry. Nothing will happen until I get back."

Only two seconds later, a call came in.

I answered, "911. What is your emergency?"

"You've got to help me." A shrill female voice.

I tried to think of how Donna responded to her calls. Calm. Methodical. "What seems to be the problem?"

"Someone has kidnapped me."

Kidnapped? Not the usual call to the FPD.

"Help me." Her voice escalated up a notch beyond shrill. Closer to a screech than a trill.

The console showed a form of pertinent information. The first space: LOCATION.

The computer automatically records the address unless the caller isn't using a landline.

LOCATION: Blank.

"I don't know." Her voice sounded terrified. "I think I'm in a basement."

Should I type that in? I wondered. I glanced behind me, praying to see Donna coming back.

The caller screamed, "You have to help me."

"Can you give me any idea where you might be? The street address. The type of neighborhood. Can you describe the house where you're being held?"

"No. Oh, God. He's coming. If he finds me with a phone, he'll…"

"Okay. Don't worry."

I scanned all the blank white spaces waiting for data. I then spied Desc, with the largest area of white for fill-in. My fingers stumbled over keys, trying to record my questions and her responses. "Just keep talking as long as you can." Tap…tap…tap… Making periods where I couldn't remember what I said, or what I asked. "Can you give me a description of the man who took you?" …tap…tap…"The type"…tap……"of the car he was driving?"

"NO! Let me go. Get away!"

Then a male voice. "Sorry. Wrong number."

Another scream, this one you'd hear in a horror movie. Or screech by a tiny mouse caught by a big cat.

My fingers froze.

The connection went dead.

Donna came back into the office.

"Thank God you're back," I scrambled out of her chair. "Someone called. She said someone kidnapped her."

Donna stood and stared, giving me the Donna-eye.

"No, honest. I tried to enter what I could."

Donna saw what was on the screen of her console. She waved me away. Took her chair like a captain taking the helm of a ship. Her fingers flew over the keyboard, filling in the blanks.

I grappled with what the girl had said. I tried to remember precisely what she told me. "She's in a basement."

Donna played her keyboard like a concert pianist. "She gave you no other information?" she asked.

And I continued to panic. "Can't you dial 86, 69, or one of those numbers to call her back?"

Her fingers stopped. "Not if she called using a cell phone." She hit some keys and scrutinized her monitor. "Looks like the call came from over on the south side."

She picked up the radio. "Chief, we may have a possible 207 in process. We have a ping from the south side of town."

The Chief ordered, "Notify all cars to canvas the area."

"Copy that."

"Caller?" The Chief asked.

Donna turned to me. "What name did the caller give you?"

"Name?" I echoed.

"Who's that with you?" the Chief asked.

"Lillian," Donna told him.

"Lillian? Did Lillian take the call?" He said it not as a question but as an accusation.

Donna mumbled, "Yes, sir."

"Report this to Lieutenant Manville. I am five minutes from the office."

"Copy that," Donna said.

"And Donna?"

"Yes, sir?"

"Make sure Lillian doesn't leave."

CHAPTER THREE

Donna's fingers continued to tap on her keyboard. She got on and then radioed what she'd put on the screen: POSSIBLE 297. FE-MALE. HOUSE WITH BASEMENT.

Was she going to get heck by the Chief for letting me answer the dispatch lines?

I gave her and the Chief some privacy so they could start investigating the call without my further interruption.

While Donna was busy on her computer, I quietly stepped back and left the station.

I hadn't driven more than a few blocks before pulling to the curb. I was trembling. I pounded the heel of my hand on my forehead, "Why hadn't I asked for a name? Stupid. Stupid. Stupid." And then I heard the voice, *No. Don't. Let me go. You're hurting me.*

I shuddered my next breath. Who was she? Where was she? And who kidnapped her and why?

If I could have done the morning differently, I'd have slept in. I'd have gone to Discount straight-on. And most definitely, I would have called Donna from the store instead of coming to the station.

Damn, Dahlia.

Damn, life—always giving me bumps on the smooth road to happiness.

CHAPTER FOUR

B ack at Oaks Manor, I saw Nelly on the phone at the reception desk. I walked over and whispered, "Have you seen Dahlia?"

While listening to her call, she shook her head. Nelly's good at multi-tasking.

"What room is Mrs. Goyen in?"

She clutched the phone between her ear and shoulder. She reached for a pencil. "Yes, that's right. We have a room vacant." She wrote out 25 on a piece of paper and nodded to me without interrupting her phone conversation. "He can move in by this weekend if that's soon enough for you." I wrote on the pad, Have A Good Day!

I headed to the corridor Dahlia had entered. I found room 25. The door stood ajar. I pushed it further open and was greeted by a thin, small, grim-faced woman lying quietly in bed. A soft, white blanket covered her. Her white hair, combed tight to her head, blended with the white of her pillow, causing her face to appear thin and elongated. Her skin, translucent, accentuated her high cheekbones. I could tell Mrs. Goyen had once been a beautiful woman. But aging and illness had double-crossed her. The only feature that kept the beauty of her youth was her jeweled sapphire blue eyes.

Dahlia had taken off her coat and stood by the sliding glass door to a small patio. Outside, rose bushes were budding. Columbines in small bunches offered purple splashes of color. Crocus dotted the flower bed, yellow, pink, and red. Apparently, Mrs. Goyen could afford a private room with a garden view. Nice.

In contrast, the white of Mrs. Goyen's bedding, the white walls, and the white-tiled floor gave the room a sterile feeling.

Mrs. Goyen squinted as if trying to make out who I was. We had never met. "Dahlia?" she summoned.

Dahlia spun around. Finding I'd arrived, she shuffled to a chair by the bed. But instead of sitting in the chair, she pulled open the seat attached to her walker. Thus, leaving the chair for me.

"Dahlia, it's getting late." I said to Mrs. Goyen, "Unfortunately, I need to pull Dahlia away from your visit."

After what happened with Donna and my gigantic blunder, I wasn't in the mood for chit-chat.

"Where do you have to go?" Dahlia challenged.

She knew good and well where I needed to be.

She signaled to the chair next to her.

I remained where I was and stretched my shoulders to remove the tightness. "The store, of course."

"Yes, I know," Dahlia said. "We'll go in a minute. But, first, Mrs. Goyen wants to ask you something."

"Oh?" I moved a little further into the room. But not too far. Something told me I should stay by the door if I wanted to make a quick exit.

Again, I could feel the muscles in my neck squeeze into a tight stranglehold.

Dahlia said flatly, "Aurelia wants you to find her husband's son."

Lying atop the cover, Aurelia Goyen's long skeleton fingers of one hand, showing swollen blue veins, twitched open and closed as if grasping to hold on to something.

I glanced from her to Dahlia and back. "I'm sorry. I..."

"Lillian will find him," Dahlia assured Mrs. Goyen. "Don't you worry, Aurelia."

Obviously, Dahlia had already committed me.

I markedly glanced at my watch. "Dahlia, we really need to go."

Dalia scowled.

Mrs. Goyen reached her calm hand over to soothe her grasping one.

There seemed something seriously wrong with Mrs. Goyen's health even if she wasn't, as Dahlia said, on her last leg.

Dahlia stood and straightened herself into an imposing force, her legs wobbling slightly, but her head held high on her shoulders. She glared over at me. Hearing an added snort wouldn't have shocked me because she stood staring me down like a bull in an arena facing its matador. I'd raised a red flag. I'd said no.

I gulped back a burp of resentment at being pushed into something I was clearly saying I didn't want to do.

"I'd think you'd want to hear her out before saying no." Dahlia's feet shuffled to steady her girth, and she leaned slightly forward, unbalanced, one hand holding the walker to keep from falling. Or maybe to keep from charging.

I glanced behind me to the doorway. Today was a morning of hasty exits.

Lord, give me strength, I mumbled under my breath.

Dahlia admonished, her hearing still perfect when you didn't want her to hear you. "Aurelia wouldn't have contacted me if this wasn't important."

"It may be my last chance," Mrs. Goyen pressed.

How do you say no to someone asking you to listen for five minutes? Someone who might be living their last five minutes?

Mrs. Goyen's hand grasped again, and her cheek twitched. I could see she was becoming stressed.

"This weekend is Valentine's Day," I tried to explain. "Even if I wanted to help you, I wouldn't have a moment free. My store is going to be busy. In fact..." I glanced behind me and took a tiny step toward freedom, "We need to be going."

"You've got plenty of time," Dahlia charged.

I took another tentative step back. Responded, "I hate opening late."

"Being late doesn't seem to bother you when it's something you want," Dahlia charged again.

"That's not true. I have customers who depend on me."

I swear, her left foot pawed the floor. Her head slightly lowered. "You run a liquor store, not a hospital."

Good lord. I stood on the threshold, unsure whether to run or stand my ground.

Dahlia shifted her feet. "We need to help. Or are you going to tell Aurelia that you can assist the police, but she's not worth helping?"

Mrs. Goyen's faint voice slurred. "It's got to be you." She laid her palms flat on the mattress and lifted herself higher on her pillows. Her head shook with the effort.

Her apparent weakness touched me. And, fearful that our arguing may cause her undue stress, I hurried over and helped settle her on her pillows.

Her dressing gown was of rich wedding satin and lace, slightly yellowed from years of wear.

"Thank you, dear," she said after I comfortably situated her. "As I have gotten older, my MS has worsened."

MS? Multiple Sclerosis. I knew little about the illness other than hearing it was a devastating disease.

Her head shaking calmed. Her grasping hand quieted. "Bernie moved me here," she said. "He couldn't take care of me at home anymore, especially with him traveling so much. Bernie was an executive for MidWestern

Bank. He was in charge of all branches and traveled extensively around Iowa." She smiled weakly. "I never blamed him for bringing me to Oaks Manor. He had little choice. My muscles had deteriorated to needing special care. Now, I can barely move."

Mrs. Goyen sighed deeply. "You're too young to have had a broken heart. Bernie's dying broke mine. And when your heart breaks, you think you will die. But, you keep living, want to or not, day after day."

"I am so sorry," I apologized.

"Oh, don't be sorry, dear. People have to do what they must in life, no matter whether they want to. That's what I told Bernie when he told me about living at Oaks Manor." She tried to smile with more enthusiasm. "When your body wars against you, you can't run from the battle."

She glanced over at Dahlia. "He was such a sweetheart, wasn't he, Dahlia? He didn't miss one day coming to see me. Why, he almost lived here."

I cast a glance at my watch.

"Will you quit looking at that damn watch?" Dahlia snapped with irritation. "Nothing is waiting for us at home except for a damn cat. So sit down and hear Aurelia out."

Mrs. Goyen's bed, arranged, angled toward the garden, was the first thing she saw on awakening. By her bed set a framed photo of a man I took to be Bernard Goyen. Golden brown skin from possibly golfing, he had nice friendly eyes with angular eyebrows, a pointed chin, and a small, well-groomed goatee—a Clark Gable look, including his ears.

The room also contained a flowered winged chair that Mr. Goyen must have brought from their home to make the room seem less like a hospital. A bureau offered a box of Kleenex, a red-clothed book, and a small crystal clock stating the time—fifteen minutes after nine.

I needed to open Discount by ten.

From her unstable condition and no wheelchair presence, I assumed Mrs. Goyen was bedridden. I also noticed there was no landline or cell phone. So I figured the lack of a phone must be why she had Nelly call Dahlia.

I went over and sat in the chair with resignation.

Mrs. Goyen hesitated, then said, "Your mother knew my Bernie. That's why she's agreed to help."

Dahlia explained, "If Aurelia was sleeping, he'd come to the television room."

"Because he knew you'd be there." Mrs. Goyen gave a ragged cough. "Dahlia, hand me a Kleenex, please?"

She continued, "I asked your mother to come today because I need to put some unresolved matters in the past where they belong." Her eyes squeezed shut. "My Bernie was a wonderful man. Everybody loved him. He was handsome and friendly, and outgoing. People couldn't resist him." Her eyes snapped open and traveled to Dahlia. "Especially the ladies."

"Now Aurelia..." Dahlia started.

Was Dahlia here to help a friend, or was she trying to make up for something? A liaison between Mrs. Goyen's husband and my mother?

I never thought Dahlia was anything but faithful to my father—even in the hard times. Late at night or early in the morning, depending on how you read the clock, she'd wake me from a sound sleep to help her drag him from off the front lawn. As a kid, I figured she only cared if he was in the house because she didn't want the neighbors talking. But in all those years, Dahlia never said a bad word about my father. And she tucked him in bed with a kiss and tenderness.

She was also not one to over-worry about other people's opinions. Whereas I thought the events at the Dove House had to be on everyone's lips.

My father died long before my brother moved Dahlia from the family home in New Liberty to a condo at the Lake View Residential Manor in Frytown. Soon after moving, two strokes took her to Oaks Manor Convalescence. And then, last winter, she attempted a great escape from Oaks Manor back to her condo at Lake View. She brought with her a man, Elmer, who had roomed down the corridor from her at Oaks.

I thought he was taking advantage of her. Maybe he gave her a little sweet talk. Or he wanted normalcy and someone to take care of him. Maybe she liked the attention. Felt young again from the sweet talk.

Dahlia spent half her savings buying new furniture and a new, younger wardrobe. Dyed her gray hair red! They might still be living together if I hadn't gotten involved with the police in the Conrad family murder. The love-crazed woman involved in the case didn't know I had moved out of Dahlia's condo and that Dahlia had returned. The woman threw a bricked chicken through the patio window. Neither Dahlia nor Elmer was badly hurt, but Elmer's children moved him closer to them. And alone and depressed, Dahlia readmitted herself to Oaks Manor. Where I found her in a convalescent bed with her red hair bleeding onto a white pillow. Dying before her time.

I couldn't leave her there because I understood her desire to reach out and grab hold of life. So, I took her to live with me.

But had Dahlia been reaching out to Bernie Goyen before moving in with Elmer?

Yuck. I didn't want to go there.

Mrs. Goyen ignored Dahlia and took the center stage back. "When you have more time than you want, memories grow closer. Some days, it's as if my room is a movie theater, and remembrances swirl around me." She reached an arm out to me. And the raking grasp of her skeleton-thin fingers sent shivers down my spine.

The woman unsettled me.

"I always thought that regretting what happened in a lifetime was fruitless," she continued. "Whatever happened, happened. Only now, feelings I once denied haunt me."

I said again, "I wish I could help, but..."

Mrs. Goyen interrupted, "I'll get right to the matter. Bernie had an affair. Maybe more than one. Men are weak. They can't control themselves. Even the best of them. I know it happened because Bernie had a child with the woman." She paused, letting that revelation sink in.

It must have been the first time Dahlia was hearing this. Her eyes grew to saucers. She nearly fell off her walker-perch.

Okay, what had Dahlia said? That Mrs. Goyen wanted me to find her husband's son? Now it made sense.

Mrs. Goyen's head shook slightly. Her thin lips formed a brittle line. "After Bernie died, his lawyer found a ledger. Bernie was sending money to the woman." She puffed a spittle retort, anger releasing. "He wanted children. We weren't able to have any of our own. But he said it didn't matter. He said we could adopt." She looked at Dahlia and said, "I wouldn't think of it. You never know what you'll get when you adopt." She paused as if what she was going to say next was difficult, but necessary. "I know he hated me for never giving him a child."

"That's not true. Aurelia, I'm sure..." Dahlia tendered.

"I'm sure..." I said, tagging along to soothe Mrs. Goyen.

But Mrs. Goyen continued, "Your mother's always telling everyone how good you are at finding out things. I need you to find Bernie's son."

I hedged. "I don't know what Dahlia has told you." Actually, I was amazed she said anything about me to her friends. If in fact, this was a friendship although strained. "But I have no talents at finding anyone. Your best bet would be your lawyer or a private detective. You could find someone in Iowa City who..."

Mrs. Goyen lashed out, "You think I'm made of money?"

I wasn't insinuating—however, a private room? She wasn't on public assistance. I asked. "I don't understand why you want to find his son. Wouldn't it be better to forget and remember your husband as..."

Mrs. Goyen didn't hesitate to interrupt. "Bernie may have been roman-tically feeble, but if I had been a healthy woman, he would never have strayed. And if his son is a good man like his father, I plan to leave our estate to him. I have no one else to leave it to. And there is no reason to punish him for his mother's sin."

A noble gesture. Yet still, a job for a lawyer, not me.

However, to make peace and to get headed off to Discount, I offered, "Okay, maybe I can make a few calls. Check the information on the com-puter. Do you know the son's name?"

"Of course. Bernard. He was named after his father."

Now, that was interesting—a child born out-of-wedlock given his fa-ther's name. Not necessarily an "of course

"Any idea where he might live?" I asked.

"They cashed the checks in Pella."

"How about the woman's name?"

"Bette Day."

I gave a pause. Not to consider the request but to give us all a moment to reflect. Then, again, I reminded myself not to get involved. "This is probably enough information for your lawyer..."

This time Dahlia interrupted, "We've already gone through this, Lillian. You need to help her."

I could have continued arguing the point. Apparently, the secret had been out to Bernie's lawyer for a long time. Why not use him? But I wanted to get going. I put my hands up in surrender. "Okay, I'll do a little research." After all, how many Bernard or Bette Days could there be in a small city like Pella? It'd be only a couple of hours of work. It would satisfy Dahlia. And what happened from that point on would be none of my business.

I asked, "Do you think Ms. Day and her son know of your husband's death?"

"The checks aren't coming anymore, are they?" Mrs. Goyen retorted angrily. Was she furious at my hem-hawing or her husband's mistress?

Her noble gesture had ragged edges.

I considered backing out of my offer. But, an attendant came into the room carrying a tray. He looked to be in his twenties with his dark hair, rather long, pulled back into a "man bun." He glanced at Dahlia and then at me. He seemed surprised Mrs. Goyen had company.

"Oh, good. Michael." Mrs. Goyen cooed.

"Sorry, I'm late," he said. "But it's nice to see you have visitors." He set the tray he was carrying down on the table beside her bed. Removed a paperback book sitting on the tray. His shirt sleeve raised slightly with the movement, offering a glimpse of a tattoo—a winged angel holding a sword.

"They aren't visitors." Mrs. Goyen's tongue licked her lips. Her face warmed, and a few years faded away. "It's you who I look forward to seeing."

His eyes shyly dropped, and he coyly smiled. "I have a surprise for you." He lifted an unfolded napkin. "A sausage biscuit for my lady," he said, as if in a Shakespearean play. "Straight from the Dairy Queen."

She giggled and returned, "Me thinks you do too much for me."

He laughed. "I'll come back. Give you time to finish your visit."

"No, stay with me," she pleaded. She reached out to him, and he took her gnarled hand into his. "I was looking forward to you reading to me this morning."

"Don't worry." His voice was soft and soothing. I am not going anywhere. When I come back, I'll bring you a cup of tea. He tapped the book and said, "Then we'll see what Pip has up his sleeve next."

He made to step away. And I could see the title of the book, *Great Expectations*.

"No. Stay. They're leaving." Mrs. Goyen gave a queenly wave.

Dahlia seemed familiar with this behavior because she immediately got up from her walker and began thumping toward the door.

There was nothing more for me to do but follow.

CHAPTER FIVE

I awoke hearing my name.

I had fallen asleep in the back room at Discount after emptying boxes of inventory onto the shelves—tiring work when there were no interruptions. And so far, the day had been quiet. Valentine's Day is not like Christmas. People generally don't plan ahead.

I wiped off the embarrassment of napping and found Melvin Roth standing at the counter. "Sorry, Mel. I didn't here you drive in."

I'd never fallen asleep at work, even on the hottest, slowest days. And I'm known for having a customer's order ready by the time they get to the counter. Most customers are regulars and relatively unchanging regarding what they like to drink.

Melvin Roth comes in every couple of weeks. He's a dirty martini type of guy, and usually, when I see him pull into the parking lot, I have his bottle of Grey Goose sacked and waiting.

"Did I catch you busy in the back?" he asked.

I nodded. "It's been a little slow today. A good time to catch up on paperwork." I started putting his order together. "Got Connie's Valentine's present yet?"

He grinned big. "Sure did. Gave it to her this morning. She'll hop on a plane to spend the weekend with Annie."

Annie was their daughter. Her once boyfriend, Darrell Carter, was sentenced to two years in prison for arson and involuntary manslaughter. I was the one who found him kidnapping Meg Dillard and taking Annie with him against her protest. After his trial, Annie left for college in Boulder, Colorado. She headed off to start life anew.

"How's she doing?" I asked. I liked Annie.

We all can make bad choices. And sometimes, we don't know they are bad until they are.

"She made the Dean's list." He shook his head. "It's hard to believe she's in her third year this year."

"Time has a way of speeding by." I gave Mel the sacked Grey Goose and his credit card receipt.

After Mel left, I had only two other customers. I considered opening my computer and beginning the Goyen project, or should I say the Dahlia project, but I wasn't motivated to do something I was being rigged into doing. Plus, I was still spinning from the dispatch call I'd taken.

Instead, I called Donna.

"Who's got a birthday coming up?" I sang.

She greeted me with, "Hey girl, where did you run off to this morning? I turned around, and you were gone."

"I didn't want to be late opening the store."

"Un-huh. Or you wanted to skedaddle before the Chief showed up."

Chief Charles Kaefring and I had been dating on and off for a while.

"Was he angry?"

"Not after I told him what would have happened if I hadn't left my office at that exact minute."

"Good. Then, he's only mad at me." Not the best scenario, but one I could live with. I wouldn't want to get Donna in trouble.

She evaded my guilt. "Lieutenant Manville, Leveque, and the Chief are trying to figure out who made the call. By the time I left, we hadn't received a missing person's report."

She paused, "Are you sure you weren't pranked?"

I winced at hearing the name Leveque. Detective of Major Crimes for the Frytown Police Department, Jacque Leveque, was a thorn in my backside. Never hesitant to put me in bad light with Charles. Especially when it came to stuff around the station.

I asked, "Do you get many calls telling you someone's been kidnapped?"

"Always a first time." She heaved a sigh. "Even so. I feel responsible. Not to the Chief. To the girl. I'd feel just terrible if something happened to her."

"I know. Sorry. Me, too."

"You need to come in and write everything down, Lillian."

"But, aren't dispatch calls recorded?"

"You know they are, hon. But you worked here long enough to know the way things go. A formal written statement is required in a situation like this."

My written statement would be compared to the dispatch call. It was called official cross-checking. Or triple paperwork—dispatch's recorded call, Donna's statement, and mine.

"I'll go down."

"Good. You best get it done right away. So you don't forget anything."

How could I forget? "I'll head there as soon as I close the store."

I went ahead and made dinner plans with her for Friday night. She loved the idea of going to Louise's Italian, saying she'd eat some extra raisins so she could feast on pasta.

After the call, I went to turn the store sign to CLOSED. Just as a pickup truck nosily drove into the parking lot. It gave a loud bang of backfire before the driver's door opened, and a small, older man hopped out.

I waited to turn the sign and went back behind the counter.

Wearing a misshapen cowboy hat low over a face harvesting grizzled grey whiskers, he came in, glancing around as if taking in the store setup before shuffling to the counter. As he came over, he tugged off a glove.

"Can I help you?" I hadn't seen him around before.

"Bet you can, sweetheart." He winked.

Usually, I'd play along with a man his age. His acting a little flirty when his chances of scoring were well below zero. But I wasn't in the mood. "I was just about to close."

"Workin' here all by yourself?"

I replied, "My husband's taking out the trash before we leave." I hated using the "husband" equation. But the question gave me some unease.

He took his hat off so he could inspect the shelves behind me. His hair looked like it hadn't been let to breathe for a while. It was matted to his head in a slimy swirl of sweat.

He licked his dry lips before asking, "What's your cheapest whiskey?" He placed the work glove he'd been holding onto the counter. It was black with grime.

But before I could answer, he pointed beyond me. "Old Crow." He reached into his pocket and pulled out a crumpled ten-dollar bill. Stretched it out to lay it flat.

"Sorry, the price is eleven sixty-nine," I told him.

He tapped the tenner with two fingers. One nail was ragged from chewing, and both were outlined with grime.

He closed one eye. He tilted his head and smiled. "The owner always gave me a discount." His lips stretched, displaying yellowed teeth with one of his front teeth missing.

"I'm the owner," I told him.

He gave me a sideways look. "Thought you said your husband was taking out the trash?" He looked me up and down. "I ain't been around for a while," he said, "but the old guy who owns this place is a quiet man full of interesting facts and ways of saying something." He ran his tongue over his lips, "Not a gal with a ponytail."

"I emphasized, Clarence Salzman, my husband's father, has passed." And to recheck him, as if we were playing a game of chess, I said, "I worked for my father-in-law. He for several years, and I don't remember seeing you before."

I wasn't afraid of the guy. But the way he looked at me, eyelids half closed, as if needing glasses, bothered me. His clothes were filthy. And, a strong smell of ammonia stirred off him with his every movement.

His eyes steadied on me. "Name's Otis Gusta. You wouldn't have remembered if you had. I don't leave much of an impression. Besides, I keep to myself." He said, "I've come from Maquoketa. I like to take a breather before the park crowd starts up. Opens in Spring."

"Maquoketa?"

"You ain't heard of the bat caves?" he exclaimed. "Here, I thought everyone knew Maquoketa. World famous. We got more than a dozen caves up there. Some are open for visitors, but others stay closed. Liability and all." He asked, "You ever been in pure darkness, missy? Where you can't see your hand two inches in front of your face?" Seeing me shake my head, he added, "It's a spiritual experience. You know, our planet lies in pure darkness. What the scientists call black matter. And when I am inside the deepest part of the caves, where it is most dangerous except for the more experienced to go, I think of the cave as holding the secrets of the universe. It gets as dark as what they call that black matter."

He looked at the shelves behind me as if reconsidering his request. "Bats can fly in all that dark like fish swim in a muddy stream. When they fly, they make a high-pitched sound, like an ultrasound, that bounces off objects in their path."

"That's really interesting," I told him. And it was. Keeping, as he said, mostly to himself must be his way of saying he lives a lonely life.

He nodded. Grinned. And he seemed encouraged by my comment because he went on saying. "We have big caves in Maquoketa. A person exploring starts out amazed by the beauty of the cave. Then find themselves pulled by the darkness. Moving further and further inside, the cave gets smaller and smaller. A couple of years ago, two cavers got stuck in a choke point. That's where the opening's so small a person can barely squeeze through. One of the cavers got free from the choke, but the other almost died from lack of oxygen."

"Do you work at Maquoketa?" From him taking off his glove, blackened with grim, and his knowledge, I thought he might be a ranger at the park."

He laughed. "Nah. My folks were from there, and once they were gone, I'd become too addicted to leave. Been there so long, I've got to where I prefer bats." He paused as if to allow me to comment, and glanced over his shoulder toward the door. Possibly thinking he'd heard my husband come in. Or maybe checking to see if he was going to?

Suddenly, I was sorry I hadn't turned the sign to CLOSED and forgone the one more customer for the day.

He said, "Maquoketa shuts its gates to the public so the bats can sleep quietly in winter. And I have to say. I like the quiet myself."

I brought him back to the point of his visit. "So, you want Old Crow?" Because I was tired of hearing his old crow.

He gave the shelves another search. "I haven't been in these parts for a while. Good to get out and see what I'm not missing. And get a good taste of what I haven't had in a while." He paused, pointed, "How much for that there bottle of Fireball? Looks to have an inch or two of dust on it."

"Fireball?" I turned to where he pointed. Barely noticeable, a small bottle, less than a pint, set slightly behind a pint bottle of Jack Daniels. I couldn't remember marking it in inventory.

He laid his hands flat on the counter. He had muscular fingers as if he worked a great deal in the fields.

I pulled the bottle down and placed it in front of him. I had no idea what to charge. "Ten should do it."

"Nah," he challenged. "This here stuff is gut rot. Just ask that husband of yours. It should be more like a Lincoln. I tell you what. I'll give you this here tenner for this bottle plus a couple of sandwiches you got in the cooler."

I glanced down at the baseball bat behind the counter. And the shelf where Clarence had kept a gun, which I hadn't replaced after someone had broken into the store and used it to implicate me in a murder.

Besides, I hated guns.

And since I wasn't sure how handy I was with baseball bats—unlike a lot of Iowans I never played— I decided his offer sounded good. Anything to get him going.

This time, I looked toward the entrance door. "That should do it." I put my finger on the ten-dollar bill. "I'd better get out there and see what's keeping Leveque."

"That your husband's name? Leveque?" He took his eyes again to the shelf behind me, maybe thinking he could make a better deal.

I hadn't realized I'd said Leveque until I heard him say it.

"He works for the police," I told him. I wasn't sure why this old guy spooked me so much. Other than being dirtier than dirt, he seemed harmless. Just a talker. And saying Charles' name instead of Leveque's would have been more logical because of Charles and my dating. A Freudian slip? I added, "He comes at closing to help out."

The man's body weight shifted. He leaned slightly toward me. The ammonia odor was so strong I had to take a step back. And decided I was done. I told him, "Go ahead and get the sandwiches on your way out."

Hint. Hint.

He wiggled a two-finger wave. "Thanks kindly."

He took the bottle and turned, walking back to the refrigerated cooler. Chatting, "Did you know there are over a thousand different types of bats? And not all of them hibernate during the winter. Some move on to warmer climates." Opening the cooler, he pulled out two sandwiches. Then he looked slyly over his shoulder before pulling out two more.

A challenge?

He grinned. "Bats don't have many predators. Owls, hawks, and snakes eat bats. But most bats die from disease." He sucked his teeth. Said, "How much more do you need? I haven't stopped to eat in a while?"

"My gift." I felt more than generous. Anything to get him out.

He grinned. "Thank you kindly. I'll remember it, don't think that I won't."

He headed to the door while still mumbling his spiel on bats. "Yep. Some people think bats are birds, with skin connecting their wing bones instead of feathers. But bats are mammals." He stopped at the door. Turned and emphasized, "The only flying mammal." He asked, "You ever heard of a flying squirrel? And we're talking about a real one here. Not like *Rocky and Bullwinkle.*"

I wondered if that is how he captured kids' interest. Did kids still watch *Rocky and Bulwinkle*? The name of the cartoon sounded pretty old.

He continued, "Flying squirrels can only glide." His hand reached for the door. "Now, there are those people who think bats are bad. Carry rabies. And some do. But mother nature provides the good and the bad to balance out this world. Bats help with pollination. Spread the seed. Ever think of that?" He hugged his purchases to his chest so that he could put on his hat. He tipped the brim with his finger. "Sorry to hear about your father-in-law."

I waited until he'd got in his truck before going over to lock the door. And switched the sign CLOSED as soon as I saw his truck rattle down the street. He was probably a harmless old guy. Maybe insecure around women. Which explained his yammer about bats. But he made me itch with apprehension.

As I drove to the station, my mind went back to telling the old man my imagined husband's name was Leveque. Why had I said Leveque? Just a silly slip of the tongue? I wasn't attracted to Leveque's type. In fact, I was terrified of going down to the station because of the possibility of running into Leveque. He'd be all over me with his "look what she's done now..." mantra. A tired tune he sang whenever I and the police were involved.

So, when I saw the Hy-Vee grocery sign, I suddenly remembered we were out of cat food. Bacardi won't eat anything besides Feline Delight. He'll eat the feathers out of a couch pillow before he sets his jaw into any other brand name.

Feathers took me back to what Otis Gusta said, *Some people thought bats were birds.* I was one of those people.

My phone rang just as I was about to get out of the car. My first thought was Charles. But the number showed a different area code. I hit the "accept call."

"Hi, Lillian."

Molly. Charles' daughter.

Yes, Charles is married. He was honest about his marriage after I found out. He explained he couldn't get divorced, even though his wife said she would give him one. As I said, Charles is a decent guy. He's not the type of man to use words loosely. He gave a vow, and he would keep it until death do they part.

But did that allow space for me in his life? It was a question I still hadn't adequately come to terms with.

"Hi, Molly," I greeted. "What's going on?"

I didn't know she had my cell number. How did she get my cell number? Would Charles have given it to her?

"We're having a birthday party for my mother, and I wanted to invite you. My mom said she would like to meet you. I told her about how much fun we had together at Christmas." She said it all without pause as if she'd practiced beforehand.

Did Charles ask her to call and invite me? He said he wanted me to get to know his wife. He said she'd accepted his relationship with me. But why would his wife be interested in meeting me? And with Molly calling to invite me to this party, a heaviness came over me.

"Gee, Molly," I said, "I think Dahlia has plans for us this weekend."

"Are you sure?" She sounded disappointed.

"Dalia mentioned the plans this morning," I lied.

"You could bring her with you. She's invited, too."

Okay, now I knew Charles hadn't suggested Molly invite me. Dahlia, wife number one, and me in the same space was a chemical mix labeled explosive. This was an innocent invitation from a young girl having met her father's girlfriend and wanted to make her father happy.

I understood that deep-seated want to fix life.

"Sorry, Molly. Maybe some other time." We exchanged some "what we were up to chit-chat," and then I told her I had been just about to head into the grocery store when she called.

"Well, if your plans change..."

"I doubt they will, Molly. But I hope you have a great party."

Are kids today so accepting of multiple parenting that inviting your dad's girlfriend to meet their mother is no big deal?

After ending the call, I headed into Hy-Vee.

I squeak-wheeled the cart immediately to the Feline Delight aisle, where there was an array of cans labeled with delectable choices. Since Bacardi won't eat the same flavor twice, I picked one of each. Next, I wheeled over to the bread aisle, grabbed some bread, then shopped for a jar of Peanut Butter, a staple of mine. *Jiff*, of course. I won't eat any other brand. Passing the cookie aisle, I also picked up Dahlia's favorite cookies, *Chocolate Pin Wheels*. Then, I did a U-turn in the aisle and got a Lime *Jell-O* snack pack. Lime Jell-O always works for me. That or a *Snickers* bar. I carry two bars in the glove box of the car for emergencies.

I pulled into Sylvia's checkout line.

"Hey, Lillian. Getting some shopping done?" She started scanning. *Beep.*

Sylvia is a veteran checker at Hy-Vee. *Beep. Beep.* She checks as if she's performing an Olympic event. *Beepbeepbeepbeepbeepbeep.*

"Just a few things," I said, trying to keep up with her pace on the conveyor belt.

Hy-Vee and Discount are not in competition. Hy-Vee sells beer, mixers, and wine. The drinkers who come into Discount want the harder liquor.

Over the chorus of beeping, Sylvia chatted. "You just missed Donna." *Beep* "Hey, what's going on down at the station?"

Sylvia craved having a bit of newsy gossip to pass on to the next customer. I shrugged. "I have no idea."

She tilted her head and squinted her eyes in appraisal. "You may not work for the police anymore, Lillian, but everyone knows you and Chief Kaefring are in a relationship."

My cheeks grew hot. "If you call dinner having a relationship?"

She stopped scanning. "Oh, come on. Only dinner?" She grinned like a Cheshire cat.

I changed topics. "Did you check eleven cans of Feline Delight? I thought I purchased ten."

She checked her machine total. "No, only ten."

"Sorry. I thought I heard eleven beeps."

Again, she gave me a knowing smile. Nodded.

"No, ten beeps." She moved on to Donna as a subject. "Well, if I didn't know Donna better, I'd swear she was a bit tipsy. So something's going on."

"Was she buying raisins?"

Sylvia's eyes got big. Her mind was abuzz with questions. "How did you know? She bought three boxes."

I wasn't going to add to the gossip. "I think she's making Oatmeal Cookies for the Women's Club." So, Donna and her vodka diet were safe with me.

I gathered my bags and headed to the car. As soon as I got inside and started the motor, I heard:

Let me go.

No. Don't.

You're hurting me.

The voice was as close to me as if I was hearing it come over the dispatch lines.

I sat with my hands on the steering wheel as if lost. Where was she? Still in the basement? Had he hurt her?

She'd called the police to get help and got me instead. My mouth soured. I strained to keep my shame from blurring my eyes. I couldn't go back to the station. Not yet. How could I face what I'd done? While I may not have done it purposefully, a mistake of this magnitude was still beyond tragic. Causing someone to be hurt, or worse, lose their life, was felonious.

Instead of driving to the police station, I headed to Louise's Italian Restaurant, thinking I would pick something up and take it home for dinner. Dahlia likes spaghetti. And Bacardi would have his Feline Delight.

City Hall and other community buildings like the library are located on First Street and Main. From there, I followed First Street to Lakeside Drive, which parallels August Lake. An artificial lake, Frytown feeds it with fish for summer fishing and offers a small camping area for those who come into town for the weekend. I don't know why the lake was named August, except August is the most crowded time when people keep it local and come to get in the last vacation days before school resumes.

Today, however, the area around the lake was not about tourism. Turning onto Lakeside Drive, I immediately saw the whirl of lights, halos of red and blue. Chief Kaefring's SUV was parked next to Leveque's banana-yellow Corvette.

Don't hurt me.

I didn't go to Louise's.

CHAPTER SIX

Dahlia nabbed me as soon as I stepped foot into the house. "Did you find anything to help Aurelia? If you did, we should tell her right away."

I returned, "I haven't had time to look on the computer yet."

Mrs. Goyen's husband's infidelity was furthest from my mind. Definitely minor compared to what was going on down at the lake. The ambulance was there because someone was hurt. Or possibly worse, dead.

"It wouldn't take long if you'd get started," Dahlia argued. "I see you had time to go shopping." She walked over and took one of the grocery sacks out of my arms, asking, "What are we going to have for supper?"

"Feline Delight," I quipped.

Bacardi immediately yowled, jumped off the couch, and followed us into the kitchen. He curled around my legs, producing a loud motor of purrs.

Dahlia pushed air between her lips. "I'm not asking for the damn cat."

I started unloading the groceries. Dahlia went back into the living room, where I heard the click of the television and the sound of a woman's voice—a news reporter. "The police state the girl has yet to be identified."

"Do you know anything about this, Lillian?" Dahlia called out.

You're hurting me.

My head spun.

Let me go.

I pulled out the can opener to open Bacardi's dinner.

Dahlia continued to repeat loudly what she heard on the television. "They're saying the police found a girl drowned in the lake."

Thinking about what they have found, or who caused my stomach to roll. The pungent odor of day-old fish from the can I was opening elevated my conscious-stricken loathing. I dumped the fishy content into Bacardi's bowl, not taking the time I usually do to make it look appealing. Bacardi sat staring at the compacted mound. Then he stared at me with his scrunched face and big brown eyes. He waited.

"We all have choices," I told him. "Eat it or don't." Again, those big, brown eyes. I squatted down and mixed it just the way he liked it.

You're hurting me. You're hurting me. You're hurting me.

"I'm not hurting you!" I yelled.

"Who are you hurting? Is that cat all right?" Dahlia shouted.

I ran out of the kitchen. Skirted through the living room without glancing at Dahlia or the television. I couldn't bear to hear what the reporter might be announcing. How the police had discovered a dead girl thought kidnapped.

You're hurting me. You're hurting me. You're hurting me.

I wanted to sleep. Disappear. Wake up again and start the whole day over.

Hurting me...

I stood in a thicket of oaks and brambles. The air smelled bitterly of algae, dust, and the residue of small animals. I couldn't place where I was. Only the area came across as familiar and yet foreign. Like somewhere I may have been before, but I couldn't remember why. I couldn't give it a name.

"Hurt me..."

"Where are you?" I whispered.

I could feel something close to me. Smelled a stench of something long dead. Evil.

The hairs stood up on my arms. It was close. Very close. And hungry.

I watched for the movement of a leaf—a hand appearing to clear an opening.

"He hurt me...and you..."

I jolted awake.

My headache thumped like a heart beating, frantic to live. What had the girl been going to say? "You?" You what? If I finished the sentence for her, she must have been going to say: *If you wouldn't have taken Donna's chair and answered my call. If you had observed Donna in how she handled dispatch calls. You could have...he wouldn't have...*

What if I had asked her name? Would that have changed things? Could the police identify the kidnapper by having her name? Would they have found her before something terrible could have happened?

The *IFS* circled in my head. And with each round, with each *what if* I ached, feeling powerless. You can't take back a *what-if*.

I forced the nightmare away. After all, I told myself, what was on the news may have had nothing to do with what happened to me yesterday morning.

I got out of bed. In the living room, I glanced at the television. I could know for sure if I turned it on and heard the newscast. But the hearing was knowing. I wasn't ready to own up to the consequences. Instead, I hurried into the kitchen, where I spotted an empty sack of Pin Wheel cookies on the kitchen counter. Had Dahlia eaten the entire pack? Did she eat anything for dinner? At least when living at Oaks Manor, she was getting regular, nutritious meals. Although, maybe not the most delicious. Was having her live with me a mistake? A BIG mistake?

Feeling inept, I opened the refrigerator and pried off a cup of Lime Jell-O from the six-pack. The gelatin melted cool and slimy in my mouth. Then, I spotted my cell phone on the counter. A notification broke the screen photo of Bacardi: *You have seven new messages*. Listed were a message from Donna, five voice messages from Charles, and a message from Leveque.

Great. What did Leveque want? I clicked on his message first.

"You did it again, Lillllllllllllllllannnn!"

He was drunk. And loud. I pulled the phone away from my ear.

"You're trouble. Fuck, you can kiss up to the Chief all you want," he yelled. "Have a dozen kids with him for all I care. But if you come anywhere near me..." He coughed. "Yeah, yeah. In a minute. Hold on."

Who was with him? Probably one of his girlfriends. Sharon?

"You.....uuu...know, don't you? We found her. Hanna Morales. Not more than sixteen. Sixteen, Lillian. DeWade Carruthers should have gotten the needle."

His voice changed in timber, sounding even drunker... "I failed. That's what the ollll'man'll say. He said I wasn't cut out to be a Fed or a small-town cop. I'm not good enough. Guess he's...rightttt...can't go back home now..."

He was slurring more and more of his words, making it harder for me to understand him. And he was moving around, the signal erratic. He shouted to someone beyond him. "I saiddddd hang on." Then back on the phone, "Damn'ttttt. Carruthers. Just like the last timmmmme."

Was he still talking to me or someone else?

Then quiet. A car honked—several times. Whoever was with him was tired of waiting.

His voice softened. Suddenly he sobered. "I'm through, Lillian. You've won. I'm quitting. I'll never be my old man."

The call ended.

I choked. I was catching his fear and wanting to stop him from his self-flagellation.

Leveque's father was the Director of the FBI at the New York Office. Big pants to fill. Leveque's drunken rage at me hinted at daddy issues. But I wasn't sure it was Leveque's father who sent him into the midlands of the Midwest. Leveque once also shared how he'd lost his mother to cancer. Was his flight to small-town an escape from losing her? Or disappointing his father?

While Leveque had no right to rage at me, I understood what failure felt like.

I'd failed the girl on the phone.

I returned to bed.

And wept.

CHAPTER SEVEN
MONDAY, FEBRUARY 9TH

"Lillian!

I opened an eye and saw Dahlia standing over me. "What time is it?"

"Seven-thirty."

I heaved a sigh and laid back down.

"Lillian. Get up."

"What?"

A hand gently patted my shoulder. "Come on. We've got things to do this morning."

My eyes were swollen. My tongue was thick. I'd had a bad dream. So vivid...

I shook my head to clear it. "Like what?" I asked, still having a hard time waking up.

"We need to find Bernie's son." Then, she commented, "Are you okay? I heard you talking in your sleep."

My head reeled. My eyes burned. Inhale. Exhale. I moaned, "I wish I had been given a normal life. Born to normal parents."

"Why do you think we weren't normal?" Dahlia sputtered.

Had I said that aloud?

Dahlia stood by the bed. Her hands were on her hips. "Who told you that your dad and I weren't like any other couple trying to make ends meet? Everyone's got problems, Lillian. Some just have more than others."

I shivered as the warmth from my comforter ripped away.

"If you look through anyone's window, it looks as if they're living a *Father Knows Best* life," she said. She folded the comforter and placed it out of reach at the end of the bed. She said, "Everyone draws the drapes closed when it gets dark." Then she moved to the subject she cared most about today. "It won't hurt you to do this one little favor for me."

"You did it again, didn't you, Lillllllllllllllllannnn?" Leveque's slurred voice woke me fully.

I jumped out of bed. It wasn't all a bad dream. I passed Dahlia and ran into the kitchen. I grabbed my phone where I'd left it on the counter.

"When you find Bernie's son," Dahlia continued saying from down the hall.

I clicked *Voice Messages*. Yes, there was a call from Leveque. Drunk. And six messages from Charles. I should have listened to Charles' messages first. Deleted Leveque's.

I pushed *Call Back* to Charles' name. He answered the first ring. And he didn't beat around the bush. He said briskly and with a tone of command, "Lillian, you need to get in here."

"I know. "I heard on the news that they found a girl's body at the lake," I informed him. "And because of me, of my not... I mean, well, maybe if I had, if you..."

Let me go. You're hurting me.

Charles said, "The body we found had nothing to do with the call you took."

"What?" Did I hear him right? "Are you sure?"

"Yes. I'm sure."

What he was saying sounded like a foreign language. It made little sense. If the girl found wasn't the girl from the call I'd taken, then who was she?

I tried not to sound relieved. "Not the girl who called the station? You're sure?"

He replied, "Lillian, get down here and give us your statement."

"I'll be there today."

"Not good enough," Charles responded. "I'll expect you in a couple of minutes."

Minutes? "I have to open the store."

"You have plenty of time for both," he argued.

I glanced at the clock. Hands showed a little after seven.

"Okay."

I got dressed. As I headed to leave, Dahlia walked out of the kitchen wearing the red apron Charles' daughter gave her for Christmas. Had Molly called Dahlia to talk her into going to her party? Did Molly know I was lying? Dahlia demanded, "Where're you going?"

"To open the store." I wanted to keep what had happened to me at the station quiet. I added, "If I go in early, I'll have time to do a little research on the computer."

She replied, "I wish you would have got to it yesterday. Aurelia's not well."

"Nelly says she's not that sick," I reminded her.

She frowned.

I braved, "Dahlia? Did you and her husband, I mean, did...?"

"You know I'm not that type of woman, Lillian. I'm insulted that you'd think I am."

"I don't. Not really. And neither am I. I wouldn't be dating Charles if he and his wife were still living together."

Dahlia didn't look convinced. "He seems like a nice enough man." But she shook her head as if all that niceness wasn't enough. "It still isn't right, Lillian. I know it isn't easy being alone. Doing life on your own. There were days I wondered if I could take on another day, working, raising you and your brothers, seeing that your father took care of himself. There were days when I didn't like your father or any of you very much. When life gets hard, it seems everyone in it makes it that much harder."

Dahlia had worked two jobs to make ends meet. I remembered how exhausted she was when she came home. Yet, she would fold the laundry, fix dinner, and kick my butt all at the same time. Dahlia was tirelessly skilled at multitasking. Not that she ever struck my brothers or me. Her disappointment was enough.

"Why is it I can't count on you to help around here, Lilly?" she'd ask, picking up after us. "Don't I have enough to care for without picking up after those who can pick up after themselves? And when she was exhausted and irritated, she would say, "Lilly, you need to improve."

Dahlia continued, "But I swear on my life, there wasn't a day that I didn't love your dad. Bad things happen, Lillian. And life keeps presenting itself day after day.

Dahlia and I rarely spoke of the past. Bringing it up now turned the space between us into a giant bubble of quiet. It popped when Bacardi came in yowling for attention.

"Go on, then," Dahlia said. "Do what you can. And tell me whatever you find before you tell Aurelia."

CHAPTER EIGHT

Before entering the station, I checked the parking lot. The Chief's SUV and Leveque's Corvette were parked inside the wire-meshed gate. Which told me Leveque must not have acted on his late-night threat.

A past employee and they don't change the lock code often, I usually enter by the back door. This morning, however, I opened the official door for visitors.

Straight, hard chairs stood along the wall—no magazines for entertainment. People came for specific reasons: To file complaints or to offer their eyewitness statements. The lobby wasn't an area for those arrested. Arresting officers entered from the back door, out of the public's eye. Or escort those arrested to an interrogation room or the process room where the suspect would be fingerprinted and photographed.

A new face was sitting behind the reception counter, a desk I once held. A civilian position, the job didn't require any special training. Daily tasks amounted to answering general calls and forwarding them to those who could give them informed answers.

I walked up to the counter and announced my intent. "I'm here to see Chief Kaefring."

"Is he expecting you?"

"Yes. We just spoke on the telephone."

"Your name?"

"Lillian Dove."

She gave no reaction; thus, my reputation hadn't preceded me. She picked up the phone and gave my name to Peggy Hudgins, Charles' assistant.

Charles came immediately. "Lillian."

I smiled. "I told you I'd be right down."

Charles was clean-shaven, his uniform pressed, and his raven black hair made his blue eyes ocean-deep. But he didn't return my smile. Instead, he was all business this morning. "Come on back." He held open the latched entry panel in the counter.

I glanced at the lobby clerk expecting her to be watching, wondering who I was and why I was there. My curiosity when I held the job was never fully resolved until I had a coffee break with Donna. But, this clerk had already gone back to answering phone lines.

I expected to follow Charles into his office. Instead, he led me past cubicles, where the morning shift handled paperwork before going out on patrol. We passed the first of two interrogation rooms. The door to the room was closed, but through the square view window, I saw Leveque sitting across from a man who looked to be in his early twenties.

Charles opened the door to the second interrogation room. "In here, Lil."

His calling me Lil was my first hint that I wasn't in too much trouble. He always called me Lil in private.

Painted a sordid green, the interrogation rooms offer an atmosphere similar to that of emergency hospital rooms but without immediate resuscitation. Acoustic ceiling tiles keep conversations at a minimum. On one wall, a reflective window allows for exterior viewing. A recording camera is positioned high up in a corner.

A writing pad and pen had been placed on the table. Charles said, "All I need for you to do is write what happened when you took the dispatch call. Try to remember what was said and what you heard."

I took a step to immediately go over to the table and get the job done.

He stopped me, saying, "But first, I need you to listen in and tell me if who Leveque is talking to sounds like the man's voice you heard on the call."

"You think he's the one who took the girl?"

But Charles didn't answer. Instead, he turned, and I followed him to the small closed door between the interrogation rooms. When opened, the narrow space revealed two dark parallel windows and a computer system. Charles continued in and pushed a button on a console. The window towards the first interrogation room lit up. Leveque's voice came through a speaker.

The room was a twin to the room I had left. It held a table and three chairs. Only two of the chairs were being used. The face of the twenty-something man Leveque was speaking to appeared as if he hadn't shaved in days. The shadow along his chin melted into his darker, shaved hairline.

Leveque stretched his arms across the table. Palms open. No secrets here. "Come on, Randy. Nola says you abducted her and held her in the basement of your Dad's house."

"You know the girl's name?" I asked Charles. "You've talked to her?"

Charles kept his attention on what was going on in the connecting room.

The guy across from Leveque gruffed, "My name's Randall, not Randy." He rubbed his hands across his shaved head in apparent exasperation. "And I told you, she's lying. I haven't been within an inch of that bitch since we broke up a month ago. Ask anyone. Like I told you, I just got back from camping."

"When did you get back?" Leveque straightened. He picked up the pen on the yellow tablet next to him, ready to make notes.

Leveque was dressed in jeans, a shirt, and an FPD jacket. His dark hair circled below his ears, coming just short of his collar.

Randall yawned.

Was Leveque getting to him?

When working at the FPD, I learned that during interrogation, when a suspect begins showing fatigue, it means they're holding back.

Randall responded, "I didn't get to unpack or clean up before you came beating on the door. If you'd made an appointment, I might have dressed appropriately." He asked, "How should I have dressed for this slip-shod, meaningless display of policing?"

Leveque's shoulder muscles tightened. He set his pen down. "Where did you say you went camping?"

Randall sneered. "I didn't. But you've probably been there yourself. Overlook Campground outside Carrollton."

"Can anyone collaborate on that?"

Randall scratched at his face stubble. "Yeah. Ask Janice Roberts. She went with me. She had to get back for the early morning shift at Connelly's. She starts her shift at six."

"You're telling me, Randy, that you haven't been in Frytown since Friday after work, and you just returned this morning at six?"

"I said, my name is Randall."

"Oh, that's right." Again, Leveque lifted the pen as if to make a note.

"I hope you're getting this all down." Randall peered over at what Leveque was writing.

Levaeque laid the pen down.

Randall smirked. "I'll try to go slow for you. Let me know if I'm going too fast." He scratched his chin, "Let's see...we left Friday night after work.

I made a reservation at the campground. Check it out. Check her out." He grinned. "Janice is worth a good, slow look." He laughed.

Leveque frowned.

Randall tapped the table with his index finger. "I took Janice home this morning. Must have been around five." He paused when Leveque made no move to write down the time. "Got that, Detective?"

Randall emphasized the D with a hard DAH.

Leveque stayed emotionally unresponsive. "Did you go into the house with her when you dropped her off? See her parents?"

"I'm not what you call boyfriend material." Randall turned his head to the side. He sucked in his bottom lip. "Thanks to you, DAHtective Leveque."

Leveque made no comment.

"My old man should have demanded your badge. Sued you for false suspicion."

"No such thing," Leveque quipped. He added, his tone changing, lowering. "Believe me, RanDAHl. Your father was way beyond suspicion."

Randall stared boldly. "Yeah? Well, I guess that that's your fuzzy mind again." He tapped his head. Then he raised his eyes, his glance coming to the window where we were watching from as if knowing the Chief was probably listening in. "I wanted my old man to leave town, but he said he wasn't running from something he didn't do. And here we are again. You've still got him in your sights and you got it wrong. Again. Nola should be in this chair, not me." His attention went back to Leveque. "Man, I bet I can sue her. Right?"

Leveque leaned slightly over the table. "I couldn't prove your father killed those girls, at least not good enough to put him away or put a needle in his arm." He paused as if wanting to let that last thought hang a bit. "But

I'm still keeping watch. Men like him think they can't make mistakes. But no one is infallible."

Randall stayed silent for several minutes. Then he barked with laughter. "You can watch until the cows come home. My old man wasn't guilty."

While we could hear the conversation, the soundproofing wouldn't allow Leveque or Randall to hear us. I whispered to Charles, "Are they still talking about the girl who called dispatch?"

Charles answered, "Nola Cross called late last night. She said she'd escaped."

Oh, sweet relief. "Then she..."

Charles motioned for our conversation to end. I went back to Leveque interrogating Nola Cross's abductor.

The two stared across at each other. Finally, Randall looked away, breaking the moment. Leveque moved the yellow pad closer as if to remind himself to stay on point.

"Okay," Leveque said, "let me get this straight. You say you were gone for the entire weekend?"

Randall leaned back, lifting his chair onto its back legs. "Yep," he grinned. Slightly rocking the chair. "Some of us need to work for a living. In case you don't know, although you probably have a file on me like you have on my Dad, I work for Hallahan Construction."

Whether or not this was known information, Leveque made a note. Leveque asked, "And Janice Roberts will verify this same timeline?"

"Janice is at Connelly's right now. Call and ask her." He paused, sucked on his bottom lip, and said, "You can call my boss at Hallahan, too. Tell him you're the reason I'm late showing up this morning. You can believe me, you will hear from my lawyer if I lose my job."

In a low, firm voice, Leveque said, "I will be talking with Ms. Roberts."

Randall set the chair back on all fours. Pushed the chair back away from the table. "Good to know. I'll inform her of your future visit."

"Hold it. We're not done." Leveque waited for Randall to sit back down.

Randall immediately went back to his causal titter-tottering.

"What about your father? Can he confirm what time you got home?"

If Leveque thought he would get a reaction by bringing the conversation back to Randall's father, he got the opposite.

Randall casually shrugged. "As far as I know, my old man's still in Des Moines." He scratched lazily at his shirt, at the camp dirt he hadn't had time to shower off. "He said he'd be gone until Monday." And as if Leveque was unsure of the calendar, Randall said, "That's today."

Leveque remained unruffled. "Des Moines? Why?"

Randall lowered his chair with a bang. "Jesus Christ. How the hell am I supposed to know? He didn't ask my permission."

Leveque poked the bear again. "Any idea why Nola Cross would say you abducted her?"

Randall's cheek muscles quivered. He took time to settle himself, then leaned away from the table again, slipping down in his chair, easy-like, as if the question held no weight. His facial muscles relaxed into a large, toothy grin. "They can't seem to let me go. You know? I keep kicking them to the curb, and they keep yoyoing back for more. Like I told you, I threw that bitch Nola Cross to the curb. Maybe she's making this up because..." He stopped, allowing a distinct pause to emphasize his following words, "Well, I guess you could say she doesn't like sharing."

He went to rock his chair back on its two back legs, but his body position created an imbalance. "I told you. Call Janice." And the unbalanced chair tipped. He fell to the floor with a large thump. Immediately he jumped up. He was fighting mad. His face was red with rage and embarrassment. "I'm through with this bullshit." He pointed his index finger at Leveque as if it were a gun. "Next time you bring me in for questioning, you'd better have a good reason, or I'll get a lawyer and sue you and this city for harassment. My old man might put up with your intimidation, but I'm not my old man."

He put his hands squarely on the table and stared at Leveque. "Put that down in writing." Then, without another word, he went over and opened the door to the room. "Next time you knock on my front door, you'd better be ready to arrest me."

Chief Kaefring asked, "Does his voice sound like the person you heard yesterday?"

"Who is he?"

"Randall Carruthers."

Carruthers, the name Leveque mentioned in his drunken message. "I don't know. I was too nervous." I confessed, "I shouldn't have taken the call." I tried hard to remember. "But I'm pretty sure the voice I heard was lower. Older, maybe."

"You're sure?"

No, I wasn't sure. "The guy on the phone only said a couple of things. He was surprised to find the girl on the phone. When he clicked off, he said –"wrong number."

Charles shut the viewing window and led us out of the screening room just as Leveque exited the interrogation room.

Leveque caught sight of me. "What's she doing here?"

I should have waited for Charles to respond. But Leveque steeled me with such a menacing look, brows furled, nostrils flaring, I couldn't hold back.

"I was about to ask you the same question. What are you doing here, Leveque?"

"I work here. You don't," he snapped.

"But didn't you call me last night to tell me you wouldn't be coming to work this morning? I was looking forward to the reprieve."

His head jerked from me to Charles. Then back to me. "I don't know what you're talking about," he growled.

His honey-brown eyes could lighten and spark gold when he was in a good mood. Grow dark as obsidian when he wasn't.

He glared at me darkly.

Charles seemed to feel a need to explain my presence. "I asked Lillian to come in and complete her statement. While she was here, I wanted her to listen in to see if she could make the voice."

"And did you?" Leveque sneered.

Instead of responding, I headed to the room to write my statement. As I left and moved into the second interrogation room, a sting of heat stung my back.

"Look, Chief," Leveque's voice raised in temperature. I thought you said you could manage her."

I stopped. Manage?

Turning, on stealthy tip-toes, I returned to the corner of the doorway.

"She has no business answering dispatch calls. You need to get it through her head. She doesn't work here anymore."

Charles responded, not bothering to answer Leveque's quip. "Bringing Randall Carruthers in for questioning is one thing. But there's no evidence of illegal imprisonment."

Leveque didn't want to hear it. "I know he got to Nola Cross. Threatened her."

Charles countered. "That's a big stretch. And this Cross incident doesn't explain the girl we found in the lake." He paused and added, "Plus, the ME states the death maybe be a possible drowning. The autopsy's tomorrow.

There are no Carruthers' victims. Let it go, Leveque. We have nothing to tie history with what's going on here today."

"Yet." Leveque barked the word loud and hard.

The voices stopped. I thought the discussion was over. But Leveque continued, lowering his voice to the point where I needed to move so far into the threshold I feared discovery.

Leveque said, "Nola Cross may have been lucky."

"Nola Cross accused Randall Carruthers, not his father," Charles answered him. "If this girl called in a false report to get her girlfriend's revenge, she needs to be warned. Randall's right. Accusing someone falsely has consequences. We could charge her with a Class Two Misdemeanor with a possibility of a thousand-dollar fine or up to sixty days in jail."

He ordered, "Get a statement from Janice Roberts. Then follow up on the Cross story."

I heard steps walking away. And then, Charles' voice. "After you write your statement, Lillian, I want you to leave. This is police business. I don't want you involved any further."

I didn't want to reassure him that his instinct was correct. That I had been eavesdropping. But, while I may have been curious about what the two men were discussing, he didn't need to worry. There was nothing more I wanted than to stay out of trouble.

I wrote my statement. As I went over the short conversation, my ears rang with the girl's voice, *hurting me....*

I scolded myself. Quit it. She's safe.

I left my statement on the desk and made a quiet exit. The new lobby receptionist barely glanced at me. When I was crossing the street to my car, I saw a man standing as if watching the comings and goings of the station. When he caught my notice, he twisted around and continued walking down the street.

CHAPTER NINE
TUESDAY, FEBRUARY 10TH

The day was full of promise. Chilly, but lately, we'd had a spurt of warm weather, giving us the expectation winter was behind us.

As I drove, I saw pink Crocus spotting color in flower beds—a straggle of yellow Daffodils popping their heads. The promise of Spring, a season of opposites. It's the time of year when days can turn warm, but the wind still blows cold. It leads to the thought that summer is just around the corner, but it feels like winter's waiting like a wolf in the shade.

Hope can be as fleeting as a weather report.

Can we wish for better weather when mother nature is entirely out of our control? Is weather different than any of the other cycles of our life? As soon as all is moving smoothly, the temperatures drop, grey clouds smear the blueness of the sky, and what seems colorful becomes hidden from sight.

Opening Discount, I immediately busied myself by replacing the drinks in the coolers and refilling the snack racks. As I worked, my mind reviewed what happened at the FPD.

Randall Carruthers stated he was on a camping trip with his girlfriend. Carrollton is only an hour away. Could he have returned to Frytown without his girlfriend knowing? Could he have kidnapped Nola Cross and, as Leveque suggested, "got" to her, forcing her to recant her story?

Yet, Charles didn't seem persuaded that Nola Cross had been kidnapped. What did he call it, girlfriend revenge?

The front bell jingled. I looked to see Percy Hastings coming through the door.

"Ooo, wee," he sang. "Spring is right around the corner. It's gonna be a good day."

I warned, "I wouldn't pack away my down jacket yet."

He smiled. "My mom always said not to chase off today for a better tomorrow. You might miss the miracle."

"Smart, Mom."

"Miss her every day." His smile diminished slightly at the thought of his mother's passing. But his good nature quickly returned.

"She was my miracle. She gave me a good life." He walked over to the cooler.

Percy's a big guy, a little over six feet, and what some would call stocky. I admired his hands. Big as paws. And he was as gentle as a teddy bear.

I expected him to pull out a six-pack from the frig. Percy's a beer drinker. He could drink beer all day long and never appear drunk. But if you gave him one finger of whiskey, it'd knock him on his butt. Instead, he surprised me this morning by choosing a large bottle of water.

Percy placed his purchases on the counter, and I rang up two bottles of water and a couple of chip sacks. He glanced at the items he was buying and said, "Aren't you gonna ask?"

"Let's see, " I played. "Your Valentine is on a health kick, but she hasn't been able to go all-in yet. She drinks lots of water but still eats salty chips."

He laughed. "Nah. I don't have a Valentine."

"Ah, Percy. That's hard to believe. None?"

He shook his head. "Wana...want..to be my Valentine, Lillian?" His face flushed beet red.

"Sure? Why not?"

Again, his face reddened a bit more. Had he been serious behind the jest?

"Why water and chips?" I asked to change the subject.

Still looking at me red-faced from my Valentine's acceptance, he grinned sheepishly. "Ah, you're teasing me." Then, standing straighter, he said, "I was hired full-time with the street department. They had an opening, and since I've been working part-time with County all these years, I filled out an application."

"Good for you, Percy."

"Go figure they'd take me seriously." He held up a water bottle. "So, no beer until my days off. I'm not going to mess this up."

"You won't." I was happy for him. Percy is one of the good guys. Sweet. Honest. He'd take off his shirt in the freezing cold of winter to help someone else stay warm. I was rooting for him.

"I won't be able to watch the store for you, though." He thought a minute and added, "Unless it's on a Wednesday. I work Saturdays with Wednesdays off. Guess that's why they hired me. Having no social life to speak of, I don't mind having something to do on a Saturday."

The last time Percy watched over the store for me cost him a broken arm. Someone came in and trashed the store. Someone who was trying to stop me from telling federal agents what I knew about an old acquaintance from Davenport. An association from my drinking life that I would have chosen to forget. But who turned up dead on my kitchen floor?

I totaled up his items. "Aren't you missed at Gas for Less?" One of his several part-time employments.

Becoming thoughtful, he said, "Jeb and I have known each other since we were kids. And he knows I could use the money." He leaned toward me, placing his mouth behind the side of his hand, whispering, "Don't tell him I said this, but I'm better at tinkering with motors than he is." He straightened and laughed. "If he needs me, I can still help him on Wednesdays. As I said, I don't have a social life other than a basketball game on the idiot tube." His neck and cheeks reddened, and he whispered behind his hand again, "No Valentines."

I smiled. "Good thing I'm not going out of town. You know I wouldn't trust anyone but you if I needed someone to watch the store for me."

He gathered up his things but seemed in no hurry to leave. "Did you hear they found a body in the lake yesterday?"

I nodded. "It was on the television news."

"We ain't had something like that for a long time."

Was Percy referring to the victims Leveque had been talking about? "Have there been many others who have drowned in the lake?"

"Not drowned. Murdered. They suspected someone from Frytown. And there are those who say it had to be someone from out of town because it just seemed to stop. Like a tourist hightailed it out of here."

Percy continued. "They let the person they suspected here in town go, but it ruined the suspected family's reputation. And it almost cost Chief Kaefring his job."

"Chief Kaefring was almost fired?" I couldn't wrap my mind around Frytown going against Charles. Or that he would have mishandled an investigation.

"Until folks realized his hands were tied by the Federal agents who took over the case." Percy paused. "Hey, did you know Detective Leveque used to work for the FBI?"

"In New York," I said, letting him know I knew.

Percy thought about that and corrected me, "I heard he came from the Midwest office in Des Moines. If he came from New York, he must have done something wrong to get himself relocated here. We're like going to Siberia for someone from the big apple." He chuckled and made ready to leave. "I thought you two were tight from everything you've been through."

I knew everyone was aware of Charles and I dating. But I also knew there was gossip about Leveque and me. Probably started by Leveque. The guys at the police station said he notched women on his belt. They made him sound like he was wearing medals of heroism.

I am not someone's notch. And, he's a kink in my side that the best chiropractor in Iowa couldn't relieve. While events may have caused me to become involved in a couple of his cases, I never set out to get entangled in crime. Stuff just happens, taking me into the whirlwind.

I told Percy, "Really, I only know Leveque from working at the station. So I'd say we were more acquaintances than friends."

Percy frowned. "You seemed pretty close with you and him working that drug case together."

"We weren't working it together."

He grinned. "Good to know." Then, "But you're still seeing the Chief, right?"

"We have dinner occasionally."

He gave my social connections consideration, then picked up his purchases. "Guess I'd better get going. My shift's not for another couple of hours, but I don't want to be late. I like to get in early and look over the trucks."

After he left, another four or five customers came in. A couple were regulars I expected to see at least once a week. Like, Stu Boil, who stopped by to pick up his half a pint of Jack Daniels. He asked if I'd driven by the lake, and told me, "The police closed the area. I heard someone drowned."

I handed back his change. "That's what I heard."

He said, "Some things keep coming around."

"Like?"

"Well, this isn't the first time someone has been found in the lake. A few years ago, someone was killing young girls. Tossing their bodies in the lake."

Stu owned the fishing tackle shop not far from the lake.

I went a little fishing. "I never heard of someone murdered at August Lake." I continued to act uninformed. "Are you saying you think those past incidents are connected to the girl they found drowned last night?"

"They're claiming a drowning, but I don't believe in coincidences," he returned. "From what I'm hearing..."

And I was happy to listen.

"...they're saying it's drowning, but far from it. And if Chief Kaefring wants to keep his job this time, he'd better nip this in the bud. Fast."

"The last person was never caught? You blame Chief Kaefring?"

"It's his job to keep this city safe. If he'd done his job, this girl yesterday might still be alive."

Stu left shorty, continuing to grumble about the lack of successful crime-solving by the Frytown Police Department. I had heard his shop was broken into last summer, and the culprit was never found. Guess he had a right to be upset.

People want answers when sometimes there are only questions. And the question utmost on my mind was why Charles hadn't come up with the solution to who was murdering girls six years ago. And what evidence had they had on their suspect?

The customers who came in after Stu wanted to make purchases quickly instead of stopping at Hy-Vee: like milk, pop, and refrigerated sandwiches.

The day was slow after the morning rush. I pulled out my computer. I wanted to get my mind off what was happening at the lake. And, the best way to get Dahlia off my back was to tell her I tried finding Mrs. Goyen's husband's son but didn't have any luck. I figured an hour on Google would produce that result.

Mrs. Goyen said the son's name was the same as the father's. A little weird when the child had been born out of wedlock. And she mentioned the last checks were cashed from Pella.

Many sites offer White Pages information, like a current phone number or address. But they all cost money. It didn't sound like Mrs. Goyen would pay for my services or expenses. Didn't she say she was using me because she didn't want to pay for someone professionally? So, with no obligation to do more than a general Google search, I put into the search bar:

Pella Iowa Bernard (Bernie) Day

The first site offered obituaries in Pella, but no Bernard or Bernie Day was mentioned. Next, two site listings provided information on the city of Pella. A photo showed windmills, appearing as if I was looking at Amsterdam instead of a town an hour and a half away. *America's Dutch Treasure!*

Many folks in Iowa don't travel far from its borders, especially overseas. Farm people can't take time away from cattle or crops, so having a place advertised as a little bit of Europe must be a big draw.

I skimmed the information on the city's Dutch history. Things to do: Windmills, Dutch architecture, Klonkkenspeal. Whatever that was. And a Tulip Festival. The page on the types of food choices gained most of my interest: Poffertjes, Friites, Oliebollen. Interesting. They also mentioned Bologna. I've lived most of my life eating Bologna or Peanut-Butter sandwiches. But, I was more interested in the types of food I couldn't pronounce. Like, *Poffertjes* tiny Dutch pancakes called to me.

I continued scanning sites. The last site on the second Google page caught my interest. It was an article from the *Pella Press*, dated January 18th:

Bette Day announces a new project for the Pella Historical Society. "I plan to dig deeper into our wonderful city's history by collecting its stories of the past as well as more photos like we have achieved and hold in the museum.

Pella Historical Society & Museums was started in 1935 by a group of dedicated Pella citizens with a passion and vision to preserve the history of Pella.

"While a picture is worth a thousand words," Ms. Day continued to explain, "someone's story gives us not only a snapshot but a deeper understanding of those who came before us."

I called Dahlia. "Can you check something for me with Mrs. Goyen?"

"Why?"

"I found something I need to verify."

"You're investigating?" She choked and coughed, the excitement of my doing something she asked almost giving her a heart attack.

"Not investigating," I corrected. "I said I would do a bit of computer research. That's all I'm going to do. So keep your blood pressure down."

"What'd you find?"

"I didn't find Bernie's son if that's what you think. But I ran across a name. Bette Day."

Dahlia sucked in air. "Oh, my. You found them, and so quick."

I would need to throw cold water on her before she called Oaks Manor. "No," I emphasized the negative loudly. I found a name. It may not mean anything. I need you to make sure I have the name right."

"Bette Day," Dahlia returned. "There's nothing wrong with my memory. I don't need to call. When you go there, you can…"

"I'm not planning to go anywhere." I reasoned with her, as I was reasoning with myself. "Pella is a long way to go. I can't just be taking off across the country bothering people who may not want to be bothered."

"But, you've got to. How else will you know? Besides, Pella isn't across the country."

"You said I had the name right. There can't be that many Bette Days in Pella, Iowa. Mrs. Goyen can hire her lawyer to do the rest."

"Lawyer? She's not made of money."

I immediately thought of Mrs. Goyen's private room. Not cheap. And she was worried about leaving an inheritance. Which meant there was some money, probably more than I had.

"I have the store to look after, Dahlia. I can't just close and take off."

"You've done it before when you needed," she spat.

"That was different."

"I don't know how."

The bell in the store jingled. "I've got to go. Call and tell Mrs. Goyen we couldn't find information on her husband's son but that a Bette Day does seem to live in Pella. Let her lawyer handle it from there. I don't know why she didn't go to him instead of me, anyway."

"Lillian, you've got to…"

"Yes, I do. I've got to go. I have a customer."

I envisioned Dahlia standing in the kitchen, her hand gripping the wall phone as if her hands were around my neck. Hanging up on Dahlia was not acceptable.

I hurried out front and found Mrs. Atkins waiting patiently at the counter. It surprised me to see her because Mrs. Atkins is a bi-Wednesday customer. This was Monday.

"Sorry, Mrs. Atkins, I was on the phone."

"No worries, dear." She was wearing a deep rose velour pants suit with a white cotton collar that accented her creamy white, always-wear-a-bonnet complexion.

"You look like Spring today." I reached for the small bottle of apricot brandy she generally purchased."

"Warm but still a bit chilly for someone my age. But it does give us hope." She said, "Not the brandy today, dear."

Mrs. Atkins drank apricot brandy and purchased Harvey's Bristol Cream for her husband. She once said a little drink while watching the nightly news helped their digestion.

"I like the embroidery," I nodded to the stitched image of two birds building a nest on her chest.

She looked down. Then up, smiling. "Love is in the air." She added, "Valentine's Day is Saturday. I was doing a few errands and thought I would beat the rush. Something special for Paul this year."

"And what might that be?" I turned and looked at the bottles stacked on shelves behind me. Most customers come to Discount for whiskey, vodka, and other harder liquors. But, I kept a few sherries and wines for those who had always purchased them from here instead of stopping at Hy Vee.

Before I could suggest something, she offered her own. "I read where Dry Sack Sherry is good."

I nodded. "It's more expensive, but lots of people like it."

"Well," she grinned. "It is Valentine's Day, and who knows how many more of those days Paul and I have left to enjoy. Might as well break the bank." She giggled.

I pulled one of my two bottles of Dry Sack off the shelf. I wiped off the dust. "I'm sure you have years of Valentine's Days ahead. I hope he's surprising you with roses and chocolates."

This brought on a blush. "He does every year," she said. "I knew the very minute I met Paul that he was a keeper."

She said, giving a shiver, but this time not from the weather. "Did you hear about the girl they found at the lake?"

I nodded.

"Poor thing. Hearing it brought back some old fears. I pray time isn't repeating itself."

I was just about to coax her into talking more about those old fears when she gathered up her merchandise. "You have a good Valentine's Day, Lillian."

After she left, I busied myself with tidying the store and going over accounts. And then I sat down and opened my computer. My mind was on Mrs. Akin's comment, calling her husband Paul, a keeper. Was there a telling sign when you found that one special person you could spend the rest of your days with? Until death do us part? When Mr. Goyen died, Mrs. Goyen learned he'd had an affair and a child. How would that feel, after years of thinking you were the only one, to find the one you have devoted yourself to had been keeping secrets? Plus a huge secret—a child.

If she and Mr. Goyen married young, that meant they'd been together for fifty-sixty years. While I get the itch to get married now and again, the thought of being tied down to one person for a lifetime cinches my throat tight, overwhelming. Plus, did I want to spend the rest of my life married? So far, my most serious life relationship has been with Vodka and my many nights down at the Candlelight Bar and Grill in Davenport, Iowa.

And how had getting married worked out for Charles? His wife became ill and couldn't be part of his life anymore. Okay, he had Molly, but she spent most of her life with his sister.

I knew Charles wanted a serious relationship, but he also made it clear he had taken his vows seriously. I wouldn't ask for him to give his wife a divorce, although she stated she would grant one. He said she wanted him to continue his life. She loved him that much. But, with that strong of a commitment still between him and his wife, and Molly involved, was there room for me? And what were my feelings for him?

I looked down and wiggled my wedding ring finger. Good lord. I was thirty-eight. What had I done with all that time?

I regretted now calling Dahlia right away. Maybe the article on Bette Day had nothing to do with Mr. Goyen. Why was I doing this research? I closed the computer. Opened it again. I put in another search: Longest time married:

According to the Guinness World Records website:

Herbert Fisher and Zelmyra Fisher from the USA hold the record for the longest marriage. The couple, who got married in 1924, lived together for 86 years and 290 days until Herbert Fisher died in February 2011.

What did they have to keep them together for eighty years?

I don't know what any of us would do without Google. It's made its fame by becoming a word in the Merriam-Webster dictionary. Verb: I google, you google, we are googling. It almost sounds naughty.

Still no customers. And I was getting bored. I typed in a new search: August Lake+body found.

I read a couple of news sites. There was also a YouTube video from a spectator who filmed the ambulance crew taking a black body bag away on a stretcher. The site claimed three thousand views—a third of the Frytown population.

Quit it, I admonished myself. I needed to stay away from this subject. So, I went back to Googling Pella.

I skimmed the Pella Chamber of Commerce's site:

Visit Pella!

Home of the Veneer Windmill. The tallest working grain windmill in the United States. Visit a city center featuring architecture reminiscent of the

Netherlands. Historical Village, including a blacksmith shop, wooden shoe-maker shop, puppet theater, church, bakery, and childhood home of Wyatt E arp.

Okay, the store bell hadn't rung once since I'd sat down at the computer. And, Pella was only an hour and a half from Frytown. I considered the absurdity of going. Finger counted the pros and cons. Look at the clock again. Listened for someone to come into the store and stop me from making a bad decision.

Out of the question. I had work to do here. I closed the computer and got to work. I tidied the shelves and racks. I rechecked the inventory and estimated what I would need to order after the holiday. That finished, I clocked the time and saw no more than an hour had passed—two long hours until closing.

I rethought the possibilities. I could close early. Go and get back before it gets too late.

A flood of guilt washed over me. Clarence never missed keeping store hours. No vacations. No sick days. His only time off was when he hired me part-time. And he never missed opening until he became deathly ill with the flu.

I had negated his stalwart discipline only once when Percy took over for me one weekend. Percy had said that since the store still opened and closed on time by using him, I still upheld Clarence's promise to his customers.

I remembered Clarence once said that Discount's hours were like a marriage vow. When made, the commitment was expected to be kept.

Charles popped back into my mind. I shook my head. I gave another glance at the clock. I reasoned that I was closing just two hours early.

I opened my computer again. I typed in Iowa Public Record and entered Bette Day's name into the search mechanism. The search offered an address for twenty dollars. I put it on my credit card number, hoping Mrs. Goyen might be good for twenty. The last known address: 1339 W. 2nd Street. Telephone number 514-555-1073.

I shut off the lights, flipped the sign in the window to CLOSED, and headed out.

CHAPTER TEN

I kept my eyes forward when passing the police station. However, I happened to glance in my rearview mirror, which is necessary for driving safely. I couldn't help but notice the parking lot was empty. All except for a banana-yellow Corvette. Leveque's car.

He didn't use his personal car a lot on police business. On duty, he'd use a cruiser. I guess the Corvette's color hampered his cloak-n-dagger methods.

I wondered if he had talked to Nola Cross yet, and what he found out from Randall's camping girlfriend. Not that I was curious.

I needed to get my mind off of what was happening at the lake. Maybe having my own investigation would help keep me minding my own business. While I may not have wanted to become involved with Mrs. Goyen, or have Dahlia think I could be so easily manipulated, I was somewhat satisfied in having Bernie's illegitimate son's mystery to keep my mind off what was happening at August Lake.

I passed Gas for Less and took the Exit onto Hwy 218, heading toward the I-80. Taking the I-80 was a longer route than following the southern flow of highways to Pella and not one I'd pick if I were taking the trip for enjoyment. The scenery on those smaller highways were Iowa postcard shots. Farms with large red barns. Green pastures with white-faced cattle. However, while I'd talked myself into closing the shop early, I wasn't about to do it to enjoy myself. Instead, I needed to check out this Bette Day. Find

out if she was connected to Bernie Goyen. Then head home to my serenity.
My store. My cat. And yes, Dahlia.

Well, maybe not an idyllic serenity, but it's what I have created in my life
so far.

I relaxed. I sang along to some oldies but goodies, and I didn't begin
to have serious reservations about what I was doing until I approached
Grinnell.

Iowa small towns have massive histories. Grinnell is one of those. I
remembered taking a field trip to Grinnell when I was in school. We
were studying the Civil War, and Grinnell had historically been a stop on
the Underground Railroad. When John Brown ushered enslaved people
through to freedom, J. B. Grinnell and others in the community helped
take care of them.

If I had the time, I would have liked to have stopped to relive the field
trip. Instead, I took Hwy 163 South to Pella. I got off on the Main Street
exit and pulled into Casey's.

Like other Casey's stores, this one offered gasoline and stop-and-go
shopping. And, since I'd forgotten to eat something more substantial than
chips at Discount, I thought I'd better fill up on several levels.

The smell of fresh-out-of-the-oven pizza hit me as soon as I opened the
door to the store. Casey's has pizza, sandwiches, drinks, beer, snacks, and
candy. I checked it all out, then I went to the counter where I saw the *Buy
Pizza by the Slice* sign. Casey's offers made-by-scratch pizza crust, which is
hard to pass up. I asked for three slices of pepperoni. Emptied my arms of
the Pepsi, Snickers, and a bag of Doritos I'd already selected. And a small
bottle of water. I was hungry. It was going to be a long trip back. Plus, I'd
need to stay hydrated.

The girl boxing my pizza slices wore a Casey's apron over a white shirt. A bit of smeared pizza sauce clung to the corner of her lip as if she'd just had a break.

"First time to Pella?" she asked, maybe seeing that I was more on a tourist level than local from my shopping order. "You'll want to buy some letters, too. They're cheaper here and just as good as from some bakeries."

I must have appeared confused as I tried to associate letters with bakeries.

"They're over here." With no one else at the cash register, she showed me what she was describing. A large wire basket offered wrapped pastries labeled *Dutch Letters*. "They're filled with almond paste," she explained. "Great with morning coffee."

I asked, "Why are they shaped like an S?"

The girl smiled as if she'd expected that question. I wasn't the first tourist she'd led to the basket. "They were first sold on Sinterklaasavond. Or Saint Nicholas' Eve. But they're big sellers and sold here all year round."

Well, when in Rome. I picked up three and added them to my other items.

I munched my first S as I continued driving Main Street, following the signs to "Old Town," advertising a Vermeer windmill, a historical village, and Glockenspiel. Unfortunately, I didn't have time for sightseeing, but this might be a fun place to return to when I could take a vacation. It may be the only way I was going to get to visit the Netherlands.

I bit into the end butt of my first S with complete satisfaction. And followed the directions on my Google map from Main Street to Broadway to West 2nd Street. A white cottage-style house with black shutters and a shiny black door held house number 1339. While the yard was still winter brown, you could tell someone worked to have nicely landscaped flowerbeds and trimmed shrubs.

I gulped some *Pepsi* and watched the house. No lights on.

There was a detached garage, closed—no car in the drive.

I got out and walked up the sidewalk. A small portico covered the front porch to keep the rain off visitors. A bowl of freshly potted pansies offered a cheerful welcome. I rang the doorbell, hearing it chime inside. No footsteps. No doors opening or closing. I rang again. If Bette Day was Bernie Goyen's mistress, she was probably around his age and may be hard of hearing.

Still no answer. I walked around the house. Like the front yard, the backyard was fenced and landscaped nicely. I walked back to the front porch. Knocked again. I tried to see inside the front windows.

Then I heard, "Can I help you?"

I fell back from the window.

A neighbor had come out onto her porch. She glanced from me down to the curb where my car was parked and then back to me. She asked again, "Can I help you? This time a bit louder and without the first friendly tone.

I could understand her suspicion. I had done little to repair my vintage grasshopper green '96 Ford Mustang convertible, which I purchased at a police auction. I'd ordered a new plastic window to replace the one duct-taped when I first bought it. I just hadn't got around to putting it in. Percy offered, but I told him I could do it myself. How hard could it be? Percy did try hammering out the dents. But there wasn't anything I could do to hide the three bullet holes.

"I'm here to see Bette Day," I called to her.

"You mean Bette Goyen?"

Goyen?

"And you are?" she called over.

The name Bette Goyen kept me from answering. Was Bette Day using Bernie's name? Had he divorced Aurelia Goyen? If she was really Bette

Goyin, why didn't she use the name in the historical society article? And in Public Record, it listed her as Day.

I wasn't sure I wanted to leave my name. Actually, I hadn't formed a plan on how to approach Bette. So, I avoided the issue for now. "I'm here to see her son, Bernie."

"He doesn't live here." She said it briefly, the conversation over.

But it confirmed I was in the right place.

She added, "Her grandson sometimes stays with her, but he hasn't been around much. He has a job near Iowa City."

I explained, "I am just here for a visit. I didn't have time to call Aunt Bette to tell her I'd be driving through. It's more of a spur-of-the-moment decision."

The woman stepped off her porch and traveled closer. This time with a warmer expression. Maybe she didn't find me nefarious. Just an out-of-town relative stopping by.

I asked, "Any idea where I might find her? Or Bernie?"

She asked, still suspicious, "You mean Bette or Bernie didn't know you were coming?"

Maybe I didn't look the criminal type, but she was being careful. "I'm over from Iowa City. This is my first time in Pella."

She frowned and seemed to think about my uninvited arrival.

So, I continued to explain my reason for not calling ahead. "I am headed to Des Moines, but when I got to Grinnell and saw it was getting so late, I thought I'd stay the night here and visit Aunt Bette."

That seemed to hit the spot. "Are you Bette's niece? Or related on her husband's side?"

Again, the husband thing. Had Bernie married his mistress? Mrs. Goyen didn't look the type to take a divorce lying down. She touted Mr. Goyen's faithfulness. From what I gathered, the affair came as a shock.

Maybe Bette had taken Mr. Goyen's last name for the sake of her son. It would cause less confusion with introductions.

Or had Bernie done the unthinkable and married Bette Day illegally? If he did, Mrs. Goyen wouldn't like to hear Bernie was a bigamist.

I tried to form a believable story. "Yes, on her husband's side. But my father passed away when I was very young. So, I never really got to know his side of the family." I stopped—enough information. Too much ancestry information, and I'd dig myself a hole with no tree to plant.

"I was so sorry about your uncle's passing," she said. "Bernie traveled too much. Traveling isn't good for your health."

This neighbor seemed to know Bernie. And the traveling for his career matched what I'd learned from Mrs. Goyen. Could he have managed two relationships with no suspicion?

Both of us waited for the other to continue the conversation. The neighbor won. I said, "I'm doing family history research, and I thought Aunt Bette would be helpful."

Bingo! She started walking over to me.

Family history was the tie that binds. Didn't everyone want to create a family tree? Find the royalty they were sure they'd come from. Look for heroes they could brag about.

She said, suddenly talkative, "My niece put our family tree together. I found out my family came from England back in the 1700s. One great uncle was an Earl." She wrapped her arms around her waist. "Getting cold," she shivered. "I don't know when Bette will be home. But you might still catch Bernie at his office. It's down on University Street. Day and Associates. Ada's father's family law office." That got her thinking, "Have you found any other lawyers or judges in your research?"

"I haven't got that far in my research yet." I was eager to go before she could pose another finding mission with this information on Bernie.

"Thank you for your help. I'll drop by and see if he's at his office. Maybe he'll know where Aunt Bette is."

I turned to leave.

"I'll tell Bette you were here," she said. "What did you say your name was?"

I kept walking as if I hadn't heard.

When I got in the car, I glanced back and saw she was still watching. So I pulled off and drove down the street. I grabbed my phone and typed in Day and Associates. Found the address. The website page stated the firm had been in business for over thirty-five years and specialized in family law solutions. A photo offered a portrait of Samuel Donald Day.

How ironic, I thought. If Bernie did illegally marry Bette Day, his son's career choice was worth a therapy session.

The building was not unlike other historic buildings on the street. Two stories. Brick. No lights showed in any of the windows.

I checked my watch even though the sun had dipped below the horizon.

Too late, the office was closed. What was I going to tell Mrs. Goyen about a second Mrs. Goyen? Did I even need to broach that part of my finding? She'd only asked me to find Mr. Goyen's son. And apparently, this was accomplished. Overall, I'd done my due diligence.

Suddenly, the front door of the building opened. A man came out carrying a briefcase. Dark hair, eyes, dark mustache. Good looks like his namesake. But what gave him away was his ears—Bernard Goyen Junior.

I got out of the car. Started up the sidewalk. "Mr. Goyen?"

He looked up. "Yes?"

I decided to go with the truth. "My name is Lillian Dove. I'm from Frytown. Aurelia Goyen asked me to confirm your location."

"Are you with the police?"

Strange question. "No."

"An investigator?"

And again, strange. Why would those be his first choices?

"Well, not officially." But then I added so that he might take my solicitation, "Well, maybe of a sort." I didn't bother to claim which of the "of sorts" I was referring to. And not sure, myself, what I meant.

He stood staring at me as if he expected an explanation. But he didn't seem surprised by my mentioning the name Aurelia Goyen. Which told me he knew about her.

"My father is dead, Ms. Dove," he said. "I severed any tie with him many years ago. And I want to keep it that way." His voice was stern and exact.

Which begged my next thought. How did he learn of his father's passing if he severed ties? Of course, as a lawyer, he would have access to records if he had the slightest bit of suspicion. A father who traveled for business, away days at a time, his schedule may have become hard to believe, especially when his father turned the age to retire. But there was the matter of the checks. Had Bernie Senior's lawyer contacted him? Then what was I doing here?

"I..." Questions swirled in my head.

He put his hand up and scowled. "As I said, Ms. Dove. The subject is closed. And if you persist in trying to contact me, or any of my family, I will file complaints of harassment." He turned as if to go back into his office. "Now, please. Leave these premises before I need to call our local police."

Really? Would he call the police on me?

Pella wasn't turning out to be such a friendly town.

He went back into the building. I stood, stymied.

Was he watching through a window? Waiting for me to leave before coming back out? Was he calling his mother to see if I'd stopped there? To, as he had put it, harass her.

I decided to leave for home. I confirmed this man was Bernie Goyen's son. Mother of Bette Day—Bette Goyen.

I'd fulfilled all obligations.

CHAPTER ELEVEN

I'd eaten my pizza slices and was on my second Dutch letter-- wishing I'd purchased more. I was planning to save the third S for Dahlia. I wondered what she would say about Bernie having a second wife. Should I tell her?

Dahlia turned the television off when I walked through the door. And when I told her I'd been to Pella, she wouldn't hear of me going to bed until I told her everything. I informed her of what I'd learned, but I decided not to tell her about Bernie's unconfirmed bigamy. He was dead. And Bernie Junior said he'd severed ties with his father. He was explicit in not wanting to have any further connection with him.

Bringing up the past can be more hurtful than memorable.

Dahlia wasn't happy when I told her Bette Day hadn't been home. But she seemed satisfied that I had spoken to Bernie Junior. "I have his law firm's address."

She asked, "What's he look like?"

"Like the photo of Bernie by Mrs. Goyen's bed."

"Then handsome."

I didn't comment.

"What else did you find out?" She wanted more.

"That's about it."

"Well," she demanded, "how is his address going to help Aurelia?"

"It's a valid address in case they had sent only the checks to Bette Day. Now, there is a way to contact the son. Mrs. Goyen can use his address to create her will."

Dahlia puckered her lips in concentration, then said, "Well, I'll let you tell her. She asked for you, not me."

I could have reminded her that Mrs. Goyen had told Nelly to call Dahlia. But I let it go and went to bed.

Dahlia turned back on the television. Loud enough that I heard a news-caster reporting again on August Lake.

CHAPTER TWELVE

Hurt me...

H I stood at an edge of a body of water.

Why was I naked?

Help me!

I knew I was dreaming because there was no way I'd be out in public without clothes on. But this dream was different from my usual nightmare—where I'd be on an island. This time, I knew I was at August Lake.

Clouds flowed over a new moon, taking away the waning light. I peered out over the dark water. "Where are you?" I called.

Here. Help me.

Then, I heard the splash of water—strangled garbles like someone drowning. I went to grab my cell phone, but when you're butt naked, you lack pockets. So I covered my breasts with one arm and cupped my "yoohoo" with my hand. "I can't see you," I shouted. I knew I needed to run for help, but there were no lights beyond the lake's edges. As if the area had been curtained off.

He hurt me

And then, suddenly, hands grabbed me by the shoulders. The roughness of clothing scratched my neck. I smelled a dank musk as if whoever had me hadn't showered in a while. I struggled to get away. I screamed.

A voice came into my ear. "Sorry, wrong number."

I was pushed. Hard. I stumbled. Fell into the water. I tried to get to my feet, but the water was too deep. Too dark. Too muddy. Then I saw her. She came floating toward me. Close. Closer. Her hair flowed in wet ropy tangles behind her. Her mouth hung open. She stared at me with empty eye sockets, flesh hanging. Her arm raised, wafted over, reaching out to me.

Suddenly, my lungs gasped. I could breathe. Oh, God. Thank you. Thank you. I don't want to die. And I realized someone was dragging me out of the water. A mouth enveloped mine. Air filled my lungs. An electrical spasm jolted my body as my blood began flowing to my heart.

I heard a voice say, "I thought you said you could control her?"

Was it Leveque? I opened my eyes. Everything around me was brighter, starker, and sweeter. Life. Then, I gagged. Coughed. The muscles in my body warred against my bones. I tried to get up but was held down.

"Didn't I tell you to stay away, Lil?" This time it was Charles's voice.

"I stayed away," I choked. I flipped over onto my side and coughed up bile and lake water.

Hurt me...the voice called from the lake.

I gagged again, feeling the swirling darkness of the lake pulling me back in.

"Help me!" I screamed.

I jolted awake with my imploring plea for someone to come to my rescue. I found myself on my bedroom floor, battling to get out and away from my comforter wrapped around my body. I panted from my excursion to get loose. My face was wet. I'd been crying.

My nightmares began when I moved to Frytown. Not that I only had sweet dreams when living in Davenport. My existence then was another type of nightmare. I wasn't sure why I started having them after moving. After all, I was sober now. But they could be a psychotic event from my years of drinking. Because I lacked blackouts to escape what I didn't want to face.

Usually, my nightmares included Dahlia. But this nightmare was different. Was this nightmare a warning?

Thirsty, I got up and went out to the kitchen. I vowed I wouldn't drive anywhere near the police station or August Lake again. I would call Donna and change from going to Louise's for her birthday. Instead, I'd suggest we go somewhere fancy and expensive. She'd love that. And the money would be worth it if these nightmares went away.

CHAPTER THIRTEEN

I considered going back to bed, but the thought of getting under my comforter wasn't comforting. So, I got dressed. Then, quietly, I made my way outside, started the car, and drove to the place I considered the safest-- Discount.

The streets were empty, dark, and vacant. People were still in dreamland while I was attempting to escape its opposite.

Then, surprise, I saw Charles's SUV parked in Discount's lot. What was he doing here? He knew my routine. There was no reason for him to expect me at six in the morning.

As I passed by him to park, I saw him bring a white styrofoam cup to his lips. Coincidence. Good. He must have been taking a break while keeping an eye on those rushing to work.

I'd barely put the car into park before he tapped on the driver's window. He smiled. I opened the car door and got out. I asked, "Why are you here so early?"

"Came to see you," he answered.

So, not a coincidence. "You thought I'd be here this early?"

"I didn't know you would," he said, "but I was willing to wait." He held up his cup of coffee. "I couldn't sleep last night. I had something on my mind. And I decided I needed to get it clear to take care of more important business."

I headed into the store. "Let's go inside. I'll warm the place up."

He followed me in.

I didn't bother with the store lights. Instead, I traveled into my work area and flipped on the lights. I picked up the coffeepot, and, while filling it with water, I said, "You're one ahead of me. If this is going to be a serious conversation, you'd better let me fully wake up."

He sat down at the table. We chit-chatted a bit—the nice weather, the thought that it might be nature's way of making a joke, a new calf born at his farm. As I listened to him talk, my mind raced to explain his visit. Had he somehow seen me drive past the station yesterday and thought I was sneaking around to learn more about his case? Or worse, had Leveque spotted my grasshopper gas guzzler? Like Leveque's banana-yellow Corvette, my Mustang was flashy in town. Or did Leveque hold court after I left the station yesterday, furthering his argument I should never be allowed to enter the police station again?

Well, I didn't need to get involved in their business. But keeping me from continuing my friendship with Donna seemed a little rash. Finally, Charles drained what was left of his cup. He set the empty down and said, "Molly called and told me she invited you to the birthday party this weekend."

So, that was it. Molly hadn't asked him about inviting me before making the invitation. Was he embarrassed? "Let me get you another cup." I smiled--*what will kids do next?* I started to rise and get a refill.

"No thanks, Lil. I can't stay long."

I remained sitting. Like me, I could understand how he was wrestling for a new life while having a foothold in his past. But I also felt it was a past life he didn't want to give up. He was still in love with his wife. He had been at her side all of these years. And he was keeping a connection with her despite her mental illness and her need for special care.

I had never profoundly dug into Charles' past. So, while I had questions, I kept them unasked and accepted his answers as he revealed them. And I thought he was doing the same. We never discussed my having a drinking problem. I am sure he knew because I never drank with him. When we first started dating, he would order wine for both of us. And I'd bring the glass to my lips without sipping. If he knew I had a drinking problem, I figured he'd take me off his dating list fast. Plus, I was enjoying this man's company. It was a type of companionship I never found in a bar or when waking to find someone next to me in bed whom I couldn't name. Eventually, when we'd go out for dinner, he'd order a glass of wine for himself, and I stayed to water. It became our routine without explanation. I really liked that. Not exactly hiding secrets from each other, but a clear understanding we had lived prior to meeting each other. And some of the past should stay in the past for the future to begin.

Charles emptied his coffee cup. "I'm not sure I would have told Molly not to call if she would have asked me first. If we continue seeing each other, Lil, and I bring her into our relationship," he paused, then said, "You like Molly, right?"

"Molly's great, Charles," I told him. "And I know you try to spend as much time as possible with her."

"I do. And I would like her to get to know you better." He added, "And you know I've told Rita that I am seeing you. So there are no secrets, Lil."

Rita, his wife. Until death do they part?

No secrets? None? That was saying a lot, especially since Charles was several years older than me. Because I had a bucket full of secrets that I carried around. Secrets about my father waiting for Dahlia to go to work before he'd leave for his real home, the Duck Inn Tavern. She thought he didn't head for the bar until just before she got home. I also had secreted away deep inside a feeling Dahlia cared more for him than her children.

Charles sat quietly, waiting as I sat thinking. Then, he changed the subject. "I told you to stay away from the station because I worry about you jumping into situations you can't handle."

Here we go, I thought. Leveque must have seen me drive by the station.

Charles said, "Look, Lil. I don't think you understand how your curiosity can jeopardize our work." He paused to let that settle in before moving on. "But I don't want you to stay away from me. I want a deeper relationship with you, Lil." He reached his open hand across the table. "I don't want any secrets between us."

Did I deserve someone like him? I heard Mrs. Atkins. *I knew the very minute I met Paul that he was a keeper.* Mrs. Goyen, *He couldn't take care of me at home anymore, especially with him traveling so much.* The article, *Hold the record for the longest marriage. The couple...together for 86 years and 290 days.*

My heart started pounding. My hands gripped my coffee cup, and panic washed over me. Then, before I could rethink my thoughts and ferret out exactly how I wanted to respond, I blurted, "I think we shouldn't see each other again."

"What?" He startled. "You don't mean that." His face fell from smiling. "Are you saying this because Molly asked you to the birthday party for my wife?" He took his hand back. Nodded. "Okay, grant it. Our relationship isn't normal, but you're aware of the circumstances. I haven't lied to you. You said you understood my situation. And Molly is eager to get to know you better. She knows how I feel about you, Lil. And just like I am trying to have an honest relationship with you, I have truthfully told her how I feel about you. And how I can see happiness ahead for the three of us."

Panic swelled within me. Us? Did he expect me to take a motherly position with Molly? Most of the time, I still fumbled with adulthood. I said, "You know my responsibility is to Dahlia."

He laughed. As if I was joking. "I enjoy your mother, and I know she can be a handful. Sometimes I think the two of you are more alike than different. But, Lil, she can take care of herself."

Hold it. Alike? What was he talking about?

He didn't pause long enough for me to ask. "We have people in each other's lives that will become part of our life. That's the beauty of finding each other. Of making a life together."

He wasn't offering marriage. He'd made it clear that he would remain legally married as long as his wife lived. And even if he was asking, I didn't want to get married. Marriage was no guarantee for a happy-ever-after. The Cinderella story was a myth. Anyone who knew the real fairytale could tell you Cinderella and the Prince didn't have a chance for happiness until Cinderella burned off the wicked stepmother's feet.

The only class I never skipped was my English class with Mrs. Harper. She was constantly comparing the myths of Disney to those Grimm told.

I glanced at the clock. "I have an appointment. I need to go." I got up.

Getting up abruptly from the table jarred him. "Lil, we need to discuss this."

I stood my ground. Or the soil I cultivated this morning. "No, Charles. Everything you said and offered...you're a wonderful man. And any woman in her right mind would say yes. But I can't."

"Lilly, wait."

My father called me Lilly. Hearing the nickname took me to the morning I ran away, seeking a new life, thinking everything would be swell once I left.

I heard the beep of Bob Cunningham's car outside our family home. He was waiting for me. And I thought I was in love with him. We had it all planned. We'd go to Davenport, and I'd help him become a famous musician. We'd get married. Have kids. Live happily ever after.

I saw myself tiptoeing past my parent's bedroom. The door was slightly ajar. I tried to keep away from the squeaky wooden floorboards that would awaken my mother and cause her to stop my only hope for happiness. And she would. There was no doubt in my mind. And yet, when I glanced into their room and saw her and my dad's sleeping forms, I longed to go inside. Crawl under the covers with them. Put my arms around them. And let myself go back to a time of innocence when I didn't understand loss, unhappiness, guilt, and shame. The overpowering shame that I would totally disappoint my mother when she woke up to find me gone. Proving once again that I wasn't the daughter she wanted.

There was nothing more to say except to repeat, "I'm sorry, Charles. I think it's best if we don't see each other." I said that as I left. I hurried to my car, got in, and backed out before he came to the door to see where I'd gone. Of course, I'd left without locking the store. But Charles would make sure the store was locked up tight before he left. That's the kind of guy he was. Reliable. Besides, if you can't trust the Chief of Police, who can you trust?

CHAPTER FOURTEEN

The front door of Oaks Manor was unlocked. But Nelly wasn't at reception. I waited. The usual morning sounds echoed from the corridors—good mornings, doors knocked on, food trollies traveling with squeaky wheels. No one came to the reception counter. Nor, when someone passed through the lobby, did they seem curious why I was waiting to be helped.

I decided to go on to Mrs. Goyen's room unannounced. As I moved down the corridors, attendants passed me taking care of business. I kept an eye out for Nelly. When I came to room 25, I stood shocked to find her bed empty. The bedcovers were mussed, but she wasn't in the room. I checked the bathroom, and I found it empty, too. Which didn't make sense. Mrs. Goyen wasn't ambulatory. Then, I remembered how sometimes the morning attendants took patients in wheelchairs to an oversized shower. I considered that was possibly where she'd gone.

Deciding I shouldn't be sneaking around, I returned to reception. Nelly was still missing. I considered waiting but decided I looked strange just standing there. So, instead, I headed to the television room, thinking I'd watch the morning news. See if there was anything more about what happened down at the lake. While I was staying away as Charles asked, it didn't mean my curiosity was under lock and key. He said to stay away from police business. He couldn't keep me from watching the morning news shows. Also, I could catch the weather report for the day. Both stories would give me conversational topics to talk to my customers about.

The weak morning light coming into the lobby from the windows gave a sober reality to the lives of the people staying there. Patients came to Oaks needing convalescent care or had no one to care for them. For many, Oaks Manor would be their last home. Whenever visiting, I couldn't shrug off the sense of loneliness honeycombing from one room to the next. I rarely heard laughter. Instead, soft, hushed voices whispered like mourners at a funeral. When I learned Dahlia had admitted herself back to Oaks after her condo was broken into, she went into a deep depression. For the first time in my life, I heard her say she didn't care if she lived—and she meant it.

I hadn't expected my life to offer me changes, and I often marvel at how far I've come from my first days of sobriety in Davenport to living now in Frytown. Without asking, I was given opportunities. I was making friends. Finding love, or the possibilities of love. Seeing Dahlia in that small, lonely room, in a bed she never claimed as hers, caused me to rethink my list of life's disappointments. Because what did Dahlia ever have to look forward to? She had spent her life taking care of my father. Maintaining the survival needs of my brothers and me. What did she want when she was a young girl? What did she wish for at her age now? She might have had a couple of strokes. She may be in her late seventies. But she had just as much a right to hope as I did.

Seeing Dahlia enfeebled and disheartened, I took her home without discussion. I acted without examining the consequences. Without the malice of how the decision was going to impact my life. A selfless act pinged innately without conscious thought but with the inherent unconscious natural knowing, pulling, and reminding me she was my mother. Mom. Mommy. No matter what steps I was moving through or the resentments I carried, and still did not completely understand, she didn't deserve to die alone. I didn't want her in a place that harbored people grappling with forced goodbyes.

Nelly once told me that most families only visited Oaks Manor on significant holidays. They brought flowers and gifts, and the atmosphere changed during those visits. "But, there aren't enough holidays," Nelly had said.

And after death? We bury those we love, and they become eventually forgotten in plots of land at places unduly named: Sleepy Hallow, Forever Rest, Rose Hills, and Sweet Shade. And my favorite, in New Liberty, where they laid my father to rest, Hope Cemetery.

I then thought of Mr. Goyen. Why did he spend his golden years coming every day to be with his wife? Was his avid attendance before or only after his son found out about the first Mrs. Goyen and cut ties with him? Marriage is such a sacred tradition. I wondered what Bernie Junior's feelings were when he found out. Traitored? Lied to? Did he then feel as illegitimate as the law would find him? And his mother? I knew immediately. He'd told her. Of course. Telling her was the only way to protect her should the truth ever become public. Did she then hate the man she'd loved? Considered her entire life a concoction of fantasy?

Mrs. Goyen had emphasized her husband never missed a day being with her. Did she see his attendance as a victory of sorts? Even today? Denial can be an intense disillusionment dispelling reality like an act of magic. It can allow a person to recreate a life to their liking or to ignore or explain away any consequences. A life so disguised does feel more manageable. Happier. More satisfying. Less tragic. But, it can also become resentful. Lonely. Afraid.

Suddenly, my coming to visit Mrs. Goyen took on a new purpose. I wanted her to know what I'd learned. Allow her to come to peace with the secrets her husband kept. Give her the ability to rid herself of all vexation.

I decided I'd wait until she'd had the time for a good shower. And she got a chance to get a bite of breakfast. Then, I would check with Nelly to ensure she was ready to take on visitors.

I continued to the TV room, my thoughts moving away from Mrs. Goyen to Dahlia's comment about her and Bernie enjoying TV together. And Dahlia's emphasis to Mrs. Goyen that she and Mr. Goyen's shared television viewing was their only commonality. They were innocently watching reruns of *Gunsmoke*.

Many might conclude that nothing more could happen in a place like Oaks Manor. But, I'd recently read an article about a game of "musical beds" occurring in convalescent homes. The "little blue pill" was the new male addition, and older women were dealing it out.

As I crossed the lobby, I felt good about my decision. By telling Mrs. Goyen it was like I was giving her a gift. Like a priest, I had the means to give her absolution.

I walked by the small office where patients could meet visitors privately, especially if they were conducting business matters. When Dahlia was first moved to Oaks after she got better but wasn't encouraged to move back to her condo, she'd wheel herself down to the office and call a taxi—*to anywhere but here.* If she couldn't hire a taxi, she was known to take out through the doors in her wheelchair. The room held chairs and a small couch, allowing for individual usage or for a small group. And I froze seeing Mrs. Goyen at the room's desk, talking on the telephone The door was ajar, and she was finishing a sentence. I heard her say, "Michael." Then immediately after, the tone of her voice changed from flowery sweetness to blind rage, and she shouted, "I don't care what you have to do. They aren't getting another cent of Bernie's money. Now, take care of it." She slammed down the phone. Then, she looked up. A vein in the middle of her forehead throbbed. Her jaw moved like she was masticating something too tough to chew.

I scurried around the corner like a thief. Good lord, did she see me? Although, I wasn't sure why I was so afraid she had. Only, in the office, she didn't come across as the same frail, dying woman I'd been introduced to. What did it mean? And who had she been speaking to? Her lawyer? If so, then why did she tell me she couldn't afford a lawyer? Why did she get me involved in any of this? And if she changed her mind about involving me, why hadn't she told Dahlia?

I heard the sounds of a chair scraping against the tiled floor. I pulled further into the shadows, planning to wait until a nurse was summoned to help her back to her room. Then, after an appropriate length of time, I'd visit her. Fulfill the obligation I'd made to her. I now considered telling her I heard the last bit of her conversation. I would let her know I was well aware she had contacted her lawyer and that she never needed my help. Instead, she'd sent me on a while goose chase. Wasted my time.

I hate geese. They run after you and bite. And it seemed she'd nipped me good and hard.

And if she tried to apologize? If she tried to explain that she'd re-decided to have her lawyer handle the situation after all? I'd still tell her about my trip to Pella. No reason for me to withhold information. She was probably already aware of some of it. Or was this whole ruse a way for Mrs. Goyen to get back a Dahlia? Could Bernie and Dahlia have...No, ridiculous.

Then, I spotted Nelly. She was coming around the corner of the corridor Mrs. Goyen was entering. And Nelly didn't seem at all surprised to find Mrs. Goyen ambulatory. They exchanged words. I couldn't hear what was said, but Nelly giggled and touched Mrs. Goyen tenderly on the shoulder.

Could this older woman be someone who looked like Mrs. Goyen? Older people take on similar features. One white head looked more or less the same as another. But no. I'd seen her clearly. She may not have been the waxed, pale woman I'd met in Mrs. Goyen's room, but I'd heard her distinctly on the phone say her husband's name, Bernie. And a reference to "that woman."

As soon as I thought Mrs. Goyen had progressed down the corridor out of hearing and Nelly took her place behind the reception counter, I hurried out of the shadows.

"Hey, what are you doing here so early?" Nelly greeted me as I came up to the counter.

"I'm coming to see Mrs. Goyen."

"You just missed her. She's on her way back to her room." She glanced around the lobby. "Is Dahlia with you?"

"No, just me." And then, because the thought was foremost on my mind and I couldn't hold it in any longer, I exclaimed, "Mrs. Goyen isn't bedridden."

My exclamation surprised her. "Of course, she's not. Why did you think she was?"

"She told Dahlia she was seriously ill."

"But I told you, she's fine. She is just getting over a bad cold. She does some things using a wheelchair. When she's feeling stronger, she likes to walk around the halls.

"But she has MS, doesn't she?" Her expression puzzled as if wondering why I was asking these questions. Finally, she said, "Dahlia knows Mrs. Goyen has suffered from the disease most of her life. I believe she was diagnosed when she was in her forties." She added, "MS isn't a death sentence. Someone with MS can live as long as someone without MS. The disease progresses with age. But Mrs. Goyen has been doing extremely well lately."

I tried to make my question less direct. "So, how long has she been a patient?" I figured the question was general enough that Nelly might not find it intrusive.

And she must not have, for she replied, "She's permanently lived here for almost twenty years."

Had Bernie been coming every day for twenty years? That would explain how he could go between Frytown and Pella without Mrs. Goyen knowing his every minute. But how did he handle his hectic job and spend time with Mrs. Goyen and his second family?

Nelly continued stating the services at Oaks Manor. "We offer our patients skilled care if they need our services for a short period to rehabilitate. And we have a set number of rooms for those needing skilled nursing for long-term." She said, "It's almost like living in a hotel room with nurses." Nelly picked up a grouping of files, letting me know our question-and-answer period was over.

I headed to Mrs. Goyen's room, my pace matching my anger. How had I been wholly bamboozled? Mrs. Goyen wasn't on her last five minutes. She wasn't probably close to her last five years. And had she been talking to her lawyer? So why had she needed me? The more I thought about how she'd wasted my time, the angrier I became.

The door to her room was partially closed. I peeked in and found her standing in front of the patio doors, looking out to the garden. I knocked. Loudly.

"Yes?"

I pushed the door fully open. On seeing me, her body became limp. She tittered on her legs. Fell.

I ran over. "Are you all right?"

She looked up weakly, "Yes, thank you, dear."

"I'll call a nurse." I went to leave and go call one.

But she stopped me, pleading, "Oh, please. No. I'll be fine. Just help me get back in bed."

I got her over to where she could safely sit on the side of the bed.

She said, her voice still weak, "If a nurse sees me up, I am going to get a tongue-lashing." Her eyes looked up to mine sheepishly, like a child caught being naughty.

"But, I saw you..." I began to tell her I had seen her in the office talking to someone on the telephone. That I had seen her walking about, without assistance. Only she faltered again.

"Saw me?" She whispered. "Oh, my. Please don't tell on me. I just wanted to see how beautiful the garden was becoming. It's been a long, cold winter." She smiled weakly. "There is so little joy in a day when you are old and lonely." Her body trembled. "Please, help me back in bed."

"I'll go get someone," I said after ensuring she was safely under the covers.

"No. Please no. I'll be all right." She leaned back, calming. Then, she opened her eyes and said, "You were here just in the nick of time. I'm lucky I didn't break my head open." She was trembling. She said, "I woke feeling so good this morning. The sun was coming in through the window. So sunny, like spring was just around the corner. I couldn't help myself." She tried to smile, but pain must have moved through her. She bit her lip. And then her entire body shuddered.

I didn't know what to do. Had I caused her to fall? I looked over to the door, hoping someone would come in. "You're sure I shouldn't go get someone."

She shook her head. "An attendant will be coming in soon with breakfast. I will have them give me something if the pain persists."

If getting up and around on her own exasperated her condition, why hadn't she called for a wheelchair or had someone to help her go to the office room? Why hadn't Nelly seemed concerned?

"You can walk, then?" I tendered.

She gave me a questioning glower. "I wouldn't call taking a few steps across the room to treat myself to a view of the garden as walking."

"No, I meant. But, I saw..."

She turned away. "If I could walk, I'd have headed straight out of here and back home years ago."

Why was she hiding her ability to walk when, apparently, Nelly hadn't been surprised at seeing her up? Her comment led me to say, "I've heard you've lived at Oaks Manor a long time."

She weakly nodded. "Twenty years, or thereabout. It feels like most of my life." She sighed. "MS is a devil of a disease. When I first came here, I needed twenty-four-hour care." She became thoughtful. "Bernie did his best. He tried to take care of me. At home, he hired a full-time nurse at the beginning of my illness. But I was no longer the woman he'd married. I couldn't believe he'd still love me." She said, "I didn't want to live if I had to be an invalid." She paused, then said, "Our life together was over. I wanted to move here. As I've gotten older, I've become weaker. I need more care. Some days, I can't even feed myself." She closed her eyes, and for a minute, I thought maybe she had fallen asleep. Then, suddenly, she asked, "Do you know the St. Francis prayer, Lillian?"

"I'm not Catholic nor very religious," I answered.

"Oh, you don't need to be Catholic to enjoy the words of St. Francis. I haven't been to mass in years." She said, "I don't remember the entire prayer, but it suggests loving without needing to be loved. I think that is a good way to live, don't you?"

I glanced at the book beside her bed, having at first thought it must be a prayer book. The title read: *Great Expectations.* The attendant had carried the same title when he entered her room while Dahlia and I visited.

She didn't wait for me to answer. "I thought of the prayer when I awoke this morning. I don't think I've lived my life very well. I haven't always given without wanting to receive." Her claim to understanding St. Francis seemed the opposite of what I heard when she was on the phone. "Bernie said he wanted to be with me every minute. He said he couldn't stand the thought of my being here alone." She seemed to rally. She smiled in thinking of him. Then, she said, "I hated needing him to help me physically. It's horrible to have your husband see you so helpless. Seeing me in this condition. This illness didn't make me very attractive." She paused and looked toward the patio doors. "But when I heard he'd taken on a mistress, I hated him for going on with life without me. I prayed for him to become ill. Only then could he understand. And then, I could sacrifice myself for him." Her voice faltered. She choked back a sob. "But when he died. It was like I had somehow killed him. And I thought I'd have to live the rest of my life, here, alone, and no one would ever love me again." She became quiet. "I loved Bernie. I never really meant it. I never wanted him to die." Suddenly she asked, "Do you think you can get a redo in life? I mean, I'm old. No denying my age or that this disease won't kill me one day. But I would like to have the chance to do it all differently. In what little time I do have left."

I thought I was the only one in the world to ask this question. The only one to realize how many heartbeats I had wasted.

Suddenly, her eyes jolted open. She stared wide-eyed, as if having forgotten I'd been standing beside her for the last few minutes. "Lillian, right?"

I said softly, "Yes, it's me, Dahlia's daughter."

Had her falling, an apparent attack, caused a bout of memory loss?

"How nice of you to visit." Her eyes batted as if trying to stay awake. "Have you found Bernie's son?"

"Are you all right?"

She grinned. Then she said, "Ask me no questions. I'll tell you no lies." Her thin arm lifted toward me weakly, her skeleton fingers grasping air. She said with a shallow breath. "Where's Michael? I need, Michael."

Then she shuddered, and her head fell deeply into her pillow, her eyes shut.

"Nurse!"

CHAPTER FIFTEEN

C hased away from Oaks Manor due to Mrs. Goyen's faint, and a nurse coming in asking what happened, feeling to blame, I left. I found myself pulling up to the curb in front of Connelly's and going inside for breakfast.

The restaurant held only two other customers. Their heads were bent to their cell phones, plates empty, having another cup of coffee before heading off for the day. I waited inside the doorway for a few minutes, unsure or not whether I should seat myself. Eventually, a girl toward the back called out, "Sit where you want. It's your pick." She then continued the conversation she seemed to be having with a girl sitting across from her.

I walked to the back of the restaurant where they were sitting. After all, if you want good service, you need to be at the forefront of attention. The girl who'd called out to me was wearing a Connelly's bibbed apron over her clothing. Her light-brown hair was pulled back into a ponytail, and her face was mildly sunburned. A cup of coffee was set before her on the white plastic tablecloth. Thinking she was on break, I waited for another waitress to come to take my order. Then, I heard, "He kept me for over an hour, asking the same questions over and over. And if he weren't so damn cute, I would have got up and walked out after the first five minutes." She rose and grabbed a menu from the stack on the table. "Let me get this order, and I'll be right back."

She came over to my table and handed me the menu she was carrying. "Coffee?"

"Yes, please. Her name tag read, *Always a Good Day at Connelly's,* and the name *Janice* beneath.

She left and went around to a service counter where there were an array of utensils, cups, saucers, and coffee pots. She grabbed a saucer and cup and filled it with what looked like a freshly made pot. Then, grabbing a container of cream, she headed back my way. "I'll give you a couple of minutes," she told me, setting the coffee down.

She had grey eyes that remained on the coffee, only lifting slightly but never totally taking in mine. Shy. The type of girl who would sit in the back of a classroom, quiet. A teacher would have trouble remembering her name. Or she'd stand along the wall at a school dance, watching the dancers with seemingly mild disinterest but seething with jealousy—desperately wanting to be asked. Someone like Randall, who held firm against Leveque's insinuation, believing in his self-assurance, would be a dream catch for a girl like Janice. Someone who finally saw her. Someone who would tell her she was beautiful.

"I know what I want," I said before she left. "Bacon and eggs, over easy, with sourdough toast." I watched as she went back to the service counter, then wrote something, ripped the sheet off its pad, and clipped it to a wheel. She spun the wheel around to the kitchen. Order placed, she then returned to where she'd been seated. She'd barely got sat down in her chair when the girl across from her said, "I've got to go in a couple of minutes."

"Okay. But let me finish. Where was I?"

"You were telling me what happened at the police station."

"Yeah. The good-looking cop. Although he's pretty old. He has a strange name, Lavek....Llllvk....something like that. I think he's French or something. She paused, maybe worried about making so much of a do about Leveque's looks. "He's not as good-looking as Randall. Just cute for a cop."

I sipped my coffee slowly, my eyes everywhere but moving to the side and back where I'd trained my ears.

I'd come to Connelly's unconsciously. No determined plan or forethought. That was my story, and I'd stick to it.

Janice said, "He asked if Randall and I had been camping all weekend. I told him we'd just got back this morning."

Casually, I glanced around the restaurant. Suddenly interested in its interior decoration.

"What's it matter what day you got back?" The girl across from Janice was dressed for a desk job asked. Skirt, white blouse. Small, conservative high heels. Her hair was neatly combed and was held away from her face by a tortoise-shelled barrette. She reached and fingered her dark-rimmed glasses back on her nose. If I was to guess, I'd say she and Janice had been best friends for a long time. Maybe since they first met in kindergarten. Or maybe they found each other standing side by side, waiting for a boy to ask them to dance. Eventually, maybe they formed an alliance that the dances were stupid. They stayed over and made a night of it, dishing those they knew who had gone. Eating popcorn and watching their favorite movies. Movies like *Titanic*, *Ghost*, or *The Notebook*.

Janice vented, "That bitch Nola told the cops that Randall had taken her and held her at his Dad's house."

"Why would she say that?" The girl asked, "What does Randall see in Nola Cross anyway?"

Janice held up her arms and stretched them out in front with cupped hands. "Double Ds."

The girl giggled. "Guess he's no different from most guys. Never thinking with the right head."

They both giggled.

Janice said, "I told this detective that Randall was with me and that he never left, not even for five minutes."

"Is that true?"

It was the same question I was silently asking.

Janice shrugged. "Nola said he'd taken her on Friday. Randall said he told the police we both left Friday after work. And we would have if Chuck hadn't called in sick and Mr. Connelly hadn't made me take his shift. But I know Randall went ahead without me, so we didn't lose our campsite. He called me from Carrollton as soon as he got there. And he came back for me as soon as Mr. Connelly let me leave early Saturday morning."

The girl commented, "So, Nola is a liar."

Janice seemed to hesitate. "Don't worry. Randall knows what she's up to."

"Order up," came a shout from the kitchen.

Turning slightly, I saw Janice half stand and leaned confidentially over to confide. "We got pretty drunk Saturday night. Randall talked about his mother leaving him when he was just a baby. What type of woman would abandon her only child? And how it really hurt him, how the kids at school treated him when his father was accused of killing those girls back in the day." She paused and said, "He's had a hard life." And added, "I love him to the moon and back. I'd do anything for him."

Her mentioning getting drunk Saturday night made me wonder if Randall had maybe not been by her side the entire night, like she said, for five minutes.

"I'm glad he was with you," her girlfriend comforted. "The police won't be able to do anything to him because he has an alibi."

"You got that right. And so does his dad. Randall said his dad was at some conference in Des Moines."

I peeked and saw they both were standing now. The girl was holding her purse, maybe anxious to avoid getting to the office late. But with a slight hesitation, unsure whether to bring the subject up, she asked, "Did you hear about the girl they found in the lake?"

"That's why they made Randall go to the police station. That and Nola." Janice shook her head. "The girl's probably some druggie."

A voice came from the kitchen. Louder this time, "Order up."

Janice said, "I got to get this order."

The girlfriend looped her purse over her shoulder. "I've got to get to work. Call me tonight, okay?" The friend left, and Janice brought my order, eggs, barely warm, and bacon limp.

I said casually, in order to open up chit-chat, "I heard you say you went to Carrollton camping. I love going there."

"It's not my favorite," Janice said. "I like going up to Spirit Lake more, but you have to have more than a weekend to go that far." She placed a hand on a hip. "But this weekend was Randall's. And I thought it was a good idea."

A sound came from upfront. She turned her head, and we both saw another customer come in. She pointed over to an empty table as a way of greeting. She walked back to the waitress station, apparently knowing this customer would want coffee.

As I ate, I gave some thought to what I'd heard. The story she'd told her friend and the one she chit-chatted to me, a complete stranger, didn't match. Why And what I should do with the information?

When I walked out of Connelly's, I spotted the cruiser immediately. Saw the curly dark head pop out of the driver's window. "Lillian!"

My Mustang was parked ten steps away from me getting away, but Leveque jumped out of the cruiser and made it over to me just as I was opening the car door to get in. He ran towards me like a dog on a hunt. Nose sniffing the air.

"What the hell are you doing here?" He demanded.

I swear his nose was pointed right at me, his one knee slightly bent, and his tail straight out.

"Breakfast," I returned, "What are you doing here?"

The question caused him to pause. Then, he rallied, "It's none of your business what I'm doing here. You were told to stay clear of this case."

"What case?" I couldn't help it. I batted my eyelashes at him and grinned.

"You know exactly what case."

Did I hear a growl? He was most definitely gritting his teeth, frowning. Then he said, "You don't come here for breakfast. And you damn well know Janice Roberts works here."

Causing me to frown and slightly growl back. "How do you know where I go for breakfast? Are you stalking me? And I couldn't pick Janice Roberts out of a lineup." I continued to feign ignorance. "There's a girl with a name tag inside, Janice. Is that her?"

I didn't wait for him to answer. I opened the Mustang's door. "I could care less about whatever case you're working, Leveque."

I never refer to him as Detective Leveque. Because...well, because I know my ignoring his title rattles him. And I like giving his rattle a shake now and again. Besides, this wasn't an official conversation.

"You were told to stay out of police business," he snarled.

"And I am." I got in the car. I could have told him what I learned. But I saw no reason to. Why offer to help him when he decidedly didn't need me to?

Leveque yelled out, "We're not done here." He twirled his hand, motioning for me to roll down the window.

I started the engine. And I did roll down the window, but only enough so he could clearly hear me say, "Oh, we're done here, Leveque. We are way past done."

CHAPTER SIXTEEN

Ahhhhhhhhhgh!

I pounded the steering wheel with the palm of my hand, imagining it to be Leveque's head. "I hate him."

How dare he think he could tell me what to do, I raged. He has no right to give me orders. I'm a citizen of Frytown. I can go to the police station anytime I want to. I can go to Connelly's every day for breakfast.

I caught my reflection in the rearview mirror. Nodded. And I just might, I thought.

I speeded to Discount, daring him, if following me, to stop and give me a ticket. When I got to the store, even though still an hour early, I tossed the sign to OPEN. Then I went into the workroom and opened my computer.

I googled: Frytown+August Lake+murders.

Several sites came up.

The first I clicked was a news release:

SUSPECT RELEASED IN FRYTOWN DEATHS.

The Frytown police released the only person of interest in the August Lake killings after Judge William Byrd ruled the lack of evidence for the death of five women found in the lake. One girl missing still has not been found. Citizens of Frytown and other local communities are worried: Stated Chuck Nelson, "How are we supposed to go about our daily lives when our wives and daughters are threatened?" But, according to Chief Charles Kaefring, there is no firm evidence to hold their person of interest. Chief Kaefring tried to relieve those concerned by telling the community his men wouldn't stop looking until the right person was found for this crime. He did not comment as to whether there were any other possible suspects at this time.

The second was an interview statement from DeWade Carruthers:

RELEASED AUGUST LAKE SUSPECT WRONGLY HELD THREATENS LAWSUIT.

DeWade Carruthers was released today as a suspect in the August Lake killings in Frytown. He stated upon release that he planned to sue the city of Frytown for false arrest. "I told Detective Leveque he had the wrong man. They had nothing on me other than someone saying they had seen me with one of the women. Someone who needs an eye examination. I've never been with any of those girls. I wasn't in the area. I was at a conference in Des Moines." Mr. Carruthers demands that Detective Jacque Leveque, Detective of Major Crimes for the Frytown Police, be fired. "And his boss can go out the door with him." Chief Kaefring for Frytown offered no comment.

A fuzzy photograph accompanied the interview statement. DeWade Carruthers looked familiar, but I couldn't put my finger on where I'd seen him. Although, Frytown isn't very big, only ten thousand population, so I could have seen him at the grocery or Louise's Italian. He appeared tall and muscular in this photo. His hair was cut short, accentuating his receding hairline. He sported a bushy mustache under a Romanesque nose. While smiling at the camera in this photo, his close-set eyes stared coldly, as if challenging the interviewer to call him a liar.

That challenge alone would set Leveque on his trail.

I clicked on several other random sites, but they told me a little more than I had already read. Six women, five were found at August Lake with one girl still missing.

I closed the computer, my mind buzzing with questions. Why was Leveque so sure DeWade Carruthers was guilty when there didn't seem to be any firm evidence to hold him? What circumstantial evidence did they have to suspect him? Charles wouldn't have taken him into custody if he hadn't been reasonably sure. And did Carruthers attempt the lawsuit? From what I heard this morning from Randall, I gathered either the suit didn't go through, or his father decided not to proceed.

I went back to search and entered: Carruthers sues the City of Frytown and found nothing more than the other sites I'd already read.

And then I tried to get a grip on myself.

No, I wasn't about to get involved. Only it did almost feel as if the coincidence of going to Connelly's this morning was close to fate having its way. As Leveque said, I had never ever been to Connelly's before. But seeing the restaurant and having just heard its name this morning must have triggered me to stop. And having Janice wait on me wasn't predictable. I may have unconsciously wondered who she was and unconsciously knew she would be at the restaurant. After all, her boyfriend had said he'd dropped her off. But who would have guessed a table would be vacant so close to where she and her friend were talking?

I thought back to the dispatch call I had taken. The girl, Nola Cross, said she was being held in a basement. Leveque said he thought Carruthers had held the women killed at August Lake in his basement. Could Carruthers be hunting again? And was it like Leveque said, Nola Cross just got lucky? Only that still didn't explain why Randall lied about when he and Janice left for camping.

A serial killer in Frytown was worthy of a horror story on Halloween. Or was this subject closed, kept quiet since justice for these girls was never found?

I can't say I wasn't intrigued. But I was resolute in not getting involved. Like I'd told Charles. I was merely curious. As anyone would be hearing this history in a town they had recently moved to. Or, as Frytown citizens worried, the horror was happening all over again.

I was determined to mind my own business.

While still being inquisitive.

Somewhat steadfast in my resolve not to become involved.

Yet, still pretty eager to find out more.

The bell in the store jingled. I closed the computer. Jamie Herta stood looking up at the bottles on the other side of the counter. Jamie worked at the Dairy Queen. Five foot two, short haircut, she had a cute pixie smile. I'd seen Leveque angling his body against her DQ counter. I wondered if she was one of his notches.

Didn't matter. What did I care?

"Hi, Jamie. Shopping for Valentine's or out of stock at home?" I greeted her.

"Hi, Lillian. I was surprised to see you were open already."

"I woke up early and thought I'd get the day started." I asked, "Buying for Valentines or yourself?"

"I'm not buying for me," she said. "I never drink alone. They say solitary drinking can be the start of a problem."

I could have told her I never drank alone. I was disciplined. I drank only at the Candlelight Bar and Grill with others who would rather cut their wrists than miss a night. Nothing better than keeping someone in the cups than suggesting another round. Drunks can maintain disciplined lives. The restraint aids denial.

Jamie continued, "I like to keep wine or something around in case someone comes by." She gave me a pixie-eye twinkle. "But, I do need to get something for a friend for Valentine's Day. Something special. What do you suggest?"

I couldn't help but wonder if that "friend" was Leveque. I said, "Give me a little more info. By special friend, do you mean friend, or putting my fingers up and offering silent quote marks"friend?"

She pouted me a small smile as if shying away from the question. "Friend," she said flatly. She waved my question away with her hand. "Nothing serious."

I gave it some thought, then offered, "Well, I would suggest something simple for a friend, like a Dewar's Scotch or Jack Daniels. Most men like whiskey."

And pow, she knocked me on my butt. "I didn't say the friend was male."

Her pout turned mischievous.

And my face must have said it all. I would never have guessed. I quickly shook myself out of it. I've never tasted the other side, but I didn't hold resentment toward those with discriminating tastes. I couldn't help wondering if Leveque knew of Jamie's preference. There was a side of me that hoped he didn't and continued to flirt away across the DQ counter.

"If you want something different," I said, "and I take it you do or you would be buying wine at the Hy-Vee, I would suggest vodka. But not just any vodka." I walked over to the vodka shelves and brought down two bottles. "Smirnoff offers a pink lemonade, but I prefer New Amsterdam's Pink Whitney. It's more expensive, but I like the bottle's design better, don't you?" I placed both bottles down on the counter for her inspection. Her eyes went to the Pink Whitney. Amsterdam understood its female market.

"What does pink vodka taste like?" She asked, inspecting the label.

I hadn't ever tried it, not liking sweet drinks, but I knew my friend Cressie had loved it. "It tastes similar to a lemon drop martini."

"Oooo. Yummy. I'll take this one." She pulled the Pink Whitney to her and reached in her purse to get her billfold.

I replaced the Smirnoff on the shelf. "Good choice." I went over to the register to ring her up.

She asked, "Are you still in a relationship with Chief Kaefring?"

I shook my head. "We weren't in a relationship. Just friends."

There was that word again. Friends. It carried a whole lot of meanings and connotations.

"I bet Detective Leveque doesn't know that."

I was puzzled, "Why would he want to?"

"Really?" She cocked her head like a pup that couldn't believe you were holding a doggie biscuit. "He talks about you all the time."

"He's involved," I said knowingly. "I think her name is Sharon."

"Oh, Sharon." She, too, said the name knowingly. "He and Sharon have been," she made air quotes, "friends for years. It's not serious." She added, mimicking a male voice. "Seen Lillian around? Did you know Lillian owns Discount? Isn't Lillian's mother a hoot?" She said, "When a man talks about someone all the time, she's gone further than possibly-- again, the air quote-- " friend." She added, "She's gotten under his skin big time."

"He's not my type," I stated firmly. "And my life's complicated enough with the store and taking care of my mother. I'm not looking for a relationship. With anyone."

"Your mother always makes me laugh when she comes in and orders a small cone but says she expects it to be bigger than a small cone." Janie giggled. "She means she wants me to make her a large cone and only charge her for a small one." She grinned. "Of course I do. She's so sweet?"

"Are you sure you're talking about my mother?"

"Yeah. I think so. Dahlia. Right?" Jamie said, "Last time she was in, she saw the hiring sign in the window, and she wanted to fill out an application."

How was Dahlia getting to the Dairy Queen? And what was she doing asking about a job?

Jamie pushed over the bills she'd taken out of her billfold.

I knew Jamie had lived in Frytown most of her life. And she knew everyone. So if the gossip was going around about the girl found in the lake, she would have heard it. I began where all good gossip exchanges start with the words, "You heard about the girl who drowned in the lake, didn't you?" I asked it casually. Then gave her the total for the purchase, "Twenty-eight, seventy-five, please." I took the two twenties she offered.

She nodded sadly. "Some say she drowned, but others aren't buying it. Like the other girls years ago, lots of people think she was killed and dumped in the lake." She slightly shivered. Lowered her voice, "I can't believe they didn't catch the guy then. We're all lucky more of us haven't been murdered." She added, "I read a lot of crime fiction. I spend a fortune at the bookstore every time we go shopping in Iowa City. I can't go without stopping at Prairie Lights. Have you been?"

I put the bills into the cash register as she continued. "I just finished Truman Capote's *In Cold Blood*. Have you read it?"

Hadn't everyone who liked a good murder story, I wondered. I shared, "I just finished one by James Elroy called The *Black Dahlia*. It's a true story about a woman found cut in two by a serial killer."

"Oh," Janie bubbled. "I read one like that by Steve Hodel.. He said his father was a serial killer. Can you imagine? Knowing your father was a murderer?"

I then thought of Randall Carruthers. Did he know the truth about his father? Is that why he'd been so insistent with Leveque of his father's innocence? I asked, "Any idea how the girls were killed back when the August Lake killings happened?" I gave her the change.

"Strangled," she said.

"With what?" Natural curiosity, like one crime reader asking another.

"I don't think they ever said." She put the change in her billfold and then went to take the bottle.

I help up a hand. "No, wait. I'll gift wrap it for you."

"Oh, you don't need to."

But I had already left for the workroom.

I'd shopped for boxes and wrapping paper for those who wanted to have their gifts fancy for Valentine's. After spending the money, I thought the idea ridiculous and ditched the wrapping into a cupboard. But now, I planned to get some return on my money. I grabbed a roll of wrapping and a box. Back at the counter, I took the bottle.

"You don't need to wrap it," she said as if wanting to make a quicker get-a-way.

"It'll be more like a gift and not just another happy hour," I argued. I began packing the bottle of Pink Vodka into the box. "Those girls at August Lake happened before I moved to Frytown." I taped the wrapping, red hearts, and cupids. "Did they ever find the person who did it?"

She glanced over her shoulder and then walked to the cooler. "Oh, they arrested someone," she said as she opened the refrigerated door. "But they got the wrong guy." She pulled out a bottle of water. She came back to the counter and again pulled back out her billfold.

"On me," I said.

"Thanks."

I tied on some red ribbon. I guessed Jamie to be in her early twenties, in her teenage years, when the killings happened. "Did you know any of the girls killed back then?"

She shook her head. "I knew one. Valerie Ohling. Her family has a farm outside of town. Most of the girls weren't from Frytown but from places close by. I remember my dad saying only an out-of-towner could be so vile. But you know, the guy they thought did it, right? The one they arrested and then let go? He has a way of staring at you like he wouldn't mind cutting you up and eating you for dinner. I hate serving him when he comes into the DQ." Again, she shivered. "I'm surprised his son can stand to still live with him."

I asked innocently. "Son?"

"Yeah. Randall Carruthers. Not a bad guy, but most kids, especially girls, keep their distance. You know, because of his dad."

"But I thought you said the police never caught the person who killed the girls."

"They didn't. But my dad said the stigma sticks to you like dog shit on a shoe."

She reddened slightly. "Sorry."

"No problem. I've heard worse."

She laughed.

The package decorating had finished. I fumbled for another question to ask that might keep her talking. "So, what are you reading now?" I asked.

"*The Obsession* by Nora Roberts. I love all her books. She adds a little romance to hers. Have you read it?"

"No, but next time I go into Iowa City, I'll plan to stop by Prairie Lights."

"Oh do," she gushed. "Don't you love going there? The choices are overwhelming if you like to read." She glanced at the time. "Uh-oh, I've gotta run. Thank's for the wrapping."

"Happy Valentine's Day."

After she left, I decided if I would continue learning information from my customers, And I needed to develop some questions ahead of time. I returned to the workroom and sat with a writing pad, pencil, and freshly made coffee.

1. Were the girls found in the lake six years ago strangled in any specific way? Like, with a rope. Their panties or bra? And what about the other girl missing? Where is she?

2. Where were the other five from? How far away from Frytown? Was there a connection to anyone in Frytown?

3. What was the circumstantial evidence for arresting Carruthers?

4. Could Randall have traveled from Carrollton without Janice's awareness and kidnapped Nola Cross? But why would he kidnap her and imprison her in his father's basement if his father had once been suspected of doing the same to other girls?

I thought again about how Janice told her friend that she and Randall drank a lot on Saturday night and passed out. Had they also partied hardy on Sunday night, too?

5. Why wasn't enough forensic evidence found in those cases in the past?

If the girls were kept in the basement of the Carruthers' house, and the forensics team searched, they should have found something. Most basements I've been in are dirty, damp, and...well, lucky. But a forensic crew is thorough, hairs, fingerprints. If it had been Carruthers, he couldn't be that perfect.

And,

6. Was Nola Cross lying?

The bell in the store jingled again.

CHAPTER SEVENTEEN

The store was busy until about one o'clock. Finally, enough customers came in who I knew well enough to start a conversation. Bob Cox from the post office—he liked to say—"I've worked there since just after they stopped the pony express." He'd follow up with, "Could retire, but I'm too young." He was going on sixty. "What would I do with all that time on my hands?"

Bob mentioned that he and his wife had been asked to chaperone the Valentine's Day dance at the high school again this year. "Don't have a kid in school anymore, but we always get the invite. Probably because I keep a good eye on that punch bowl." He gave an example of the steadfast eye he kept on it. And, of course, Marjorie still offers free catering. His wife Marjorie owned a bakery and catering business in town called Marjorie's Kitchen.

"Who made Sweetheart Queen this year?" I knew the Valentine's Dance crowned a Sweetheart King and Queen. But if you offered me a million dollars, I wouldn't be able to tell you who was last year's. Yet, I tried it. "Wasn't Nola Cross last year's Queen?"

"Nola Cross? Nah. She graduated a couple of years ago. I see her folks now and again. She goes to Iowa State now."

Before he left, he said, "Keep safe. From what I hear is going on down at August Lake, it's not good to go out alone after dark. Valentine's Day night needs to be canceled."

After another few customers that I didn't know well enough to start up chatty conversations came and went, Andie McDowell came in. She had a pulse on the town from serving at The Dog House, a bar and grill frequented by guys on the police force.

Andi once told me she'd thought of becoming a policewoman. Claiming, "I can kick butt as good as any man." Of which I had no doubt. She stood at least eight inches taller than me, almost six feet. It would cause a bathroom weight scale to move around more than once. And she cracked the best dirty jokes. She was a pal to most officers who went to the Dog House for a beer after a shift. So I was more than happy to see her come in this morning.

"Been busy?" She asked.

"A little more than usual," I replied, "considering it's mid-week, and there are still three more shopping days until Valentine's."

"I've never been much for that holiday," she quipped. "Men like to give you roses, but I always say you've got to watch out for the pricks."

She waited. I giggled appreciatively and asked, "Did some prick bring you roses lately?"

"Do I look like I'd suffer a prick?" She laughed. "I told my Pauly, don't bring me flowers or any of those stuffed animals. Just be ready to stuff me instead." She gave a roaring bellow of a laugh at this joke.

Although, I am not quite sure she was joking.

Paul Volk, her boyfriend. A small man about half her size. And if she ever got on top in their lovemaking, she'd squish him like a marshmallow. But there was no doubt the man worshipped the ground Andi walked on. Whenever I saw the two together, he'd look up at her as if he were gazing at a goddess.

"Have you been busy?" I asked, turning the conversation as I got her the Don Julio Blanco Tequila.

"Expect it to be a pretty slow day with the goings on at the lake."

"I heard. They found a girl."

"From what I heard, she was in for a couple of days." Andi added, "Miner said she was in pretty bad shape, with the fish having got to her."

Sergeant Mitch Miner. He was a professional and took his job seriously. And I knew he wouldn't give out any information that wasn't already spilling around town.

"Have they identified her yet?" I asked.

"Nancy Yates, from over in Tiffin. How the hell she ended up in our lake is beyond me."

"Someone told me..." I tendered, "It's the same as what happened at the lake several years ago when those girls were found."

"Killed and dumped like rubbish. There are probably six. They just haven't fished the fifth up yet." She paused and asked, "You don't remember? Scared the piss out of everyone around here. Male and female. Young and old."

I shook my head. "I didn't live here then."

"Well, it about scared the bejesus out of everyone. Those who come to use the lake may get more than snookered now and again. Maybe sticky-handed. But someone fished out murdered is not an everyday thing in our community."

"Then it's right what I heard. The girl didn't drown in an accident." Although it was a long shot, maybe Miner hinted at something.

"No, murdered."

By the time Andie left, the name Nancy Yates from Tiffin hadn't been announced on the news. Or at least, not that I'd heard. Nor was the News saying the death was anything but a drowning. What Andi had told me came straight from the Dog House.

Tiffin was a smaller community than Frytown, about three miles away. What had she been doing here?

After Andie left, I thought I'd make Friday night's reservation for Donna's celebration. I figured Louise's might not be the best choice from what was happening. I knew another of her favorite places to go shopping and for dinner was up at the Amana Colonies. An area that kept to their German influence. Then, I gave her a ring and see which was her choice.

"The Ox Yoke's yummy. I sometimes dream about their Schnitzel," she said when I told her my idea. Then I heard a hesitation in her voice. "But it's busier than a squirrel collecting nuts around here at the station. And you know how I love Louise's." She paused, then added, "And you know that Friday night's the High School Sweetheart Prom. They'll be coming into Louise's wearing their prom dresses. I'd sure hate to miss it."

I knew she was right on both accounts. She loved Louise's and enjoyed the kids. And it was her birthday. But if I was caught at Louise's with Donna? Only, who was Charles or Leveque to warn me away? I had every right to go to dinner anywhere I wanted. And if they saw me, well, so be it. I was going to mind my own business, and they could mind theirs.

"But what about the incident at August Lake?"

"Hon. Drownings happen. It won't keep people from eating."

"Bob Cox was in and said they might cancel Valentine's Day."

"People are saying a lot of things around town. But, until they cancel Valentine's Day and my birthday, I'm looking forward to celebrating."

"Okay, Louise's it is," I agreed.

"We'd better get a reservation. With the dance, it'll fill up," she suggested.

"Will do. I'll call as soon as I hang up. Reservation for maybe seven?"

"Better make it for six-thirty," she countered. "The dance starts at eight, so the kids will eat early."

As I hung up from Donna, I saw Percy's truck drive into the lot. He got out and walked in, smiling from ear to ear.

"What are you doing here? I thought today was your day off?"

"Yep, it is. But I went in this morning to give the trucks a look over before the crews went out. I don't get paid for the time, but I know the County appreciates my concern for their vehicles. And I like my job." He gave a laugh. "Haven't worked full time for years and forgot how nice it is to have a place to go when you wake up."

Percy had taken care of his mother until her death a couple of years ago. He went to the cooler and pulled out a six-pack of Bud. Brought it over to the counter.

"I was just making plans with Donna Stockman," I chatted. "Valentine's Day is her birthday. I am taking her to dinner."

"She's good people," Percy said, laying a ten-dollar bill on the counter. "I don't know what the police station would do without her."

"That's what everyone thinks," I agreed. "The officers love her."

"Most everyone in Frytown loves Donna. And boy, can she whip up a batch of cookies."

We both laughed. Donna not only spoiled everyone at the police station with her cookie baking, but hers was always the most prominent line at any baked goods sale.

I confided, "She wants to go to Louise's for her birthday dinner. She likes seeing the kids dressed up for the Sweetheart Dance."

"Louise's is a good choice. Can't beat their spaghetti."

"I suggested we go to the Amanas." I reddened. "Chief Kaefring warned me against spending time down on Lakeside."

"Why the hell did he do that?"

I shrugged. "He thinks I'll get involved with what happened to the girl found at the lake." The condition of said girl I left undefined. And waited to see what Percy may have heard down at the street department. "I told him I had no desire to get mixed up in any police business. "

"Don't see why not," Percy countered. "You have a knack for ferreting out vermin."

I laughed. Percy was no stranger to my involvement. Not after having his arm broken from sitting in for me at Discount. I said, "Vemin seem to attract to me, like the boyfriends I used to date. I've learned to stay away from that type."

"Well, if you want to go down to Lakeside, you should go," he said. "In fact, if you were to take a day off, I'd take you there myself."

His cheeks reddened. A bold declaration for shy Percy.

I tried to think of something else to talk about. My stomach growled.

Percy laughed and slapped his stomach. "Maybe I should push that offer up a bit." He said, "I heard the police say they know who the girl was they found."

I pushed the change over toward him, which he ignored. I told him, "Andi from Ox Yoke was in. She said the girl was from Tiflin. I haven't heard it on the News yet."

"Yep, that's what I heard, too. And the local news will probably catch it the same as I have. Everyone in town is talking." He shook his head. "Hope they don't find another one,"

I admitted. "I researched on the computer about the girls killed there before."

A grin pulled at the corner of his lips.

I hurried to add, "I was only interested because a lot of customers know about what happened back then. And so, I thought I should read about it so I'd know what they were talking about." Waited. Added, "I found an interview with the person they suspected."

"DeWade Carruthers," Percy named.

"Do you know him?" I asked, trying to keep more than just historical research inquisitiveness out of my voice.

He nodded."Know him, but don't like him much." This was strange because Percy generally had good things to say about everyone. If you want to know more about those girls murdered back then, you should talk to Bill Egarman. He owns the newspaper."

"*Frytown Gazette?*"

I glanced over to the small area where people could find complimentary local newspapers. The *Frytown Gazette* provided news on the local events around town. Gave updates on the latest city council meetings—and advertised sales for the week.

Percy said, "The Gazette back then covered all the news around these parts before *Midwest Reporter* took over small-town newspapers" Then, he gave me a wink. Cheeks reddened. "Since I'm off the clock, if you want to go over and talk with Bill now, he's probably in the office. And I don't mind watching the shop for you."

I shook my head. Busied myself with straightening items on the counter. "No, but thanks. I was just wondering, is all."

Percy reasoned. "He knew Clarence pretty well. So you have probably met him before without knowing it." He glanced out of the window to the parking lot. "Seems like a slow day. I'll take you for lunch if you want to close up for an hour. We could stop by the Gazette for a minute. I know Bill real well. I'll introduce you."

His forehead joined the color of his cheeks.

I was just about to decline his offer again when Percy turned and walked over to the window. He flipped the store sign, ClOSED.

"What are you doing?"

"Come on. Write a note you'll be back by three. That way, you won't miss the after-work rush." He smiled, "I know you, Lillian. You're burning to know about those girls killed back then. And Bill wrote about the murders. He writes some for the *Iowa City Press*, too. He'll be able to fill that curiosity of yours. He'll know the ins and outs of what's happening now. He went over to the door. Opened it. "Besides, I could go for a cheeseburger. Isn't Dairy Queen one of your stops?"

I argued, "My customers expect Discount to be open from nine to six, just like when Clarence was here."

He countered. "They expect you to eat something for lunch, too, now and again."

"But..."

"One hour. And if you lose a sale, I pay for it."

I wasn't sure how we'd prove whether someone came to the store in the hour when we were gone. Or know what they would have purchased. But, "Okay," I caved. "A cheeseburger sounds good. Only, let's not stop at the newspaper office. I'm not "burning" to find out about the past murders. I was just looking the case up on the Internet for something to do."

"Uh, ha. Gotcha." He came over and picked up the six-pack. "Well, are you coming?"

"Okay, give me time to write the note and lock up."

CHAPTER EIGHTEEN

Percy's Chevy Silverado was spotless inside, but my Mustang was always full of crumbs..

"I see you still haven't got that back window in your car?"

"I'm getting to it," I told him. Which was probably what I said last time he mentioned it. We headed down Wilson to Main Street.

"What's it been? Almost a year since you bought the new window?"

"I thought I'd wait until the weather was warmer. No sense putting a new window in when it's going to freeze up and crack."

"The sun ruins that material faster than the cold."

Instead of turning on Main Street toward the Dairy Queen, he turned in the opposite direction. "I'm happy to do it for you."

"You've done enough for me, Percy. I'll get to it after Valentine's Day, and the store slows down."

Although I wasn't sure where he was taking me, I was glad to see we were not heading toward the Frytown Gazette office. "By the way, lunch is on me."

"No, sir. I'll be dang if I let a pretty girl buy me something to eat." Pink cheeks. "This is all on me."

Okay, I knew Percy had a crush on me. Maybe for Percy, it went beyond a crush. And I liked him—a lot. I admired his loyalty and honesty, but there was no chemistry.. At least nothing sparking on my side.

"So, where are we going? This isn't the way to DQ." I asked to lessen the romantic tension.

We passed farm supply buildings, crossed railroad tracks, and pulled into an older section of Frytown. A residential area. He pulled up in front of an older, two-story home, painted grey some years back. With steps moving from the cracked sidewalk to another set of steps leading to a full front porch. The type was large enough for a porch swing on a hot summer night.

"I thought you might want to see where he lives," Percy said.

"Who?" Two large, windows on each side of what looked like a heavy oak door. They built this house before flimsy materials. Solid wood planks.

"DeWade Carruthers," Percy said. "His family built the house back in the 20s."

Which wasn't unusual for Frytown or other nearby small communities. Charles lived on his family's farm, which the family has owned since the late 1800s. He showed me his great-grandmother's house, still there near the farm, with a few tilts and the porch slightly off-kilter.. But Charles said with pride, "No one but family has lived here for almost a hundred years. When it comes up vacant, the family gets together and decides who will move in next. Usually, we hand the keys over to a couple newly married."

It's one of the great things about small towns. Families root them.

"Why'd you bring me here?" I asked Percy.

"I figured if you're going to learn about what happened years ago with those girls, DeWade's name will come up. "

I told him, "I told you I was just interested."

His laughter stopped me. "Everyone knows where everyone puts their head down at night. Especially if they have been laying it down at the same place since they were born."

A small black car slowed down alongside us. Randall Carruthers rolled down the driver's window. Percy did the same.

"Can I help you with something?" Randall asked. A girl was riding in the passage seat. Not Janice.

"Hey, Randall. No, we were just on our way to lunch, and I thought I would drop by and check with your Dad. He's wanted me to look at that old pickup of his. He said the transmission was giving him trouble."

"He should have driven that heap of junk to the dump years ago," Randall said. "He puts more money into it and this old house falling down than he ever spent on me."

Percy returned, "Yep, owning an antique is a big black hole to throw hard-earned money into. But, last I saw, he had it pretty pristine. Said he'd been going to car shows with it."

Randall looked toward the house as if he was done chit-chatting and in a hurry to get inside. "He won't be home until sometime tonight. He's been at a plumbing conference in Des Moines. Goes every year."

A screech came from inside his car. He jumped. "Damn, the radio keeps going in and out. Has a mind of its own." He reached over to turn it off. Then he glanced over at me. But, unless he'd been in Discount, we hadn't met. He'd left the police station before I came out of the viewing room.

He became anxious, thumping his thumb to the beat of a radio he had just switched off. "Best be getting to it," he said.

"Well, when you see your dad, tell him Percy stopped by to check out his truck."

"Will do." With that, he rolled his window back up and pulled his car into the driveway.

Percy continued down the street.

CHAPTER NINETEEN

"Percy, where are we going? I can't be gone from the store very long. I shouldn't have left."

"You left a note saying you'd be back by three. I'll have you back in plenty of time."

This time he pulled in front of a three-story brick home with lead glass windows looking out to the street.

I had driven on this street before and knew the home was considered one of the city's historic houses. It had a large wraparound front porch supported by unique brick arches. A driveway led to an old carriage porch where carriages would stop so their occupants could get out without the weather damaging their clothing. The carriage porch was elevated, and visitors would enter by a large doorway. Brick steps led to the front door, where an American flag was poled, and a plaque gave the words: WITH LIBERTY COMES WITH TRUTH.

The door opened on Percy's gentle knock.

"Percy? Well, I'll be damn. Was I expecting you?"

The man's shoulders slightly stooped as if he'd spent much time working at a desk. He had a shiny bald head with dark hair cut neatly around its crown. Wearing black, heavy frames, he looked through a thick lens with questioning green eyes.

"Nah, but you said the invitation was always open."

"And it is, of course. Only, I am a bit scheduled this afternoon."

He glanced at me.

"I'm Lillian Dove," I introduced myself. "A friend of Percy's." And when I didn't think that thoroughly addressed my identity, I added, "I own Triple A Discount."

"Oh, sorry," Percy excused his lack of introductions. "Lillian Dove, this is my good friend, William Egerman."

"Bill, please." He extended his hand. "We sure miss Clarence at our monthly poker game." He moved back, allowing room for us to enter. "Come in, come in. I'm always happy to see you, Percy."

"We don't mean to bother you," Percy said, stepping in. "But Lillian and I were talking about the historic homes around here, and I thought you might let me show her around."

The man slipped his glasses to the top of his head, and in doing so, his eyes grew smaller. He squinted at me. "You're interested in architecture?"

I stood still, trying to put together Percy telling them we'd been talking about historic homes.

"Your house is beautiful, Mr. Egerman. It's hard to imagine they built here it in Frytown instead of a larger city like Des Moines or Iowa City."

He laughed. "I don't answer well to Mr. Egerman. Please, call me Bill." He offered the entry we were standing in. "This home was my grandfather's idea of retirement. He and my grandmother moved from Chicago in 1920 after he closed his newspaper office. But with times the way they were, he started a small paper here. He said people in the country had a right to know the truth, as well as those who lived in the cities.

"The house is Italianate. It was more than what he and my grandmother needed, and far more than what my family and I needed, but at the time, it was the fashion, especially in big cities. People built large houses to show economic status. And my father started largely. But those of us who came after him couldn't continue the image he had in mind for his paper.

Chicago had big stories. Here in Frytown. Let's say our news is interesting but not exemplary."

A circular stairway offered steps to a landing, and another set of stairs circled to a second landing. Colonnades separated two rooms from the entry. I could see the room to the left ran the length of the entire front of the house. A beautiful stone fireplace centered the room's furnishings. To the right was the dining room with a long, dark wood table and a built-in china cabinet filled with colorful ceramic and glass. All the woodwork appeared to be originally varnished hardwood. And the floors and stairway were hardwood, protected with richly colored rugs.

Bill continued. "Today, it costs too much to keep the entire house heated. Martha and I keep the third floor blocked off. The ballroom on the second floor is closed as well. We don't give enough balls for the need of that room." He said, "Any other time, Lillian, I'd be happy to show you the house. Please, have Percy bring you back. But I am on an unusual deadline. The *Iowa City Press* has asked me to write up an article on this latest death we had here at the lake."

"That's another reason we came by," Percy spoke up. "Lillian heard about the lake murders, and I told her you'd be the person to talk to."

Bill scratched the top of his head, and his fingers found his glasses. He placed them back on. "I thought I'd never have to revisit those files. And yet, here I am. Reporting on a cold story that's haunted our city's past."

He explained his involvement to me. "Curtis Stokes, owner of the *Iowa City Press*," asked if I'd cover this latest. I covered the story six years ago when the first murders and missing girls started happening." He told both Percy and me, "And, from what I learned today, this girl's death wasn't an accident."

CHAPTER TWENTY

"**N**o, it can't be!"

The three of us twisted around to see where the voice was coming from. A woman in her late forties stood just inside the room. With generous, plump curves, her dark brown hair rounded her face. She was dressed layered in a long, green sweater over a pink T-shirt and jeans. On her lips, a muted but daring red lipstick.

"Percy Hastings?" She called.

Percy seemed dumbfounded. Then suddenly, his face lit up. "Barb?"

And like one of those commercials, arms stretched out toward each other as if in slow motion, they met halfway, hugging.

"What are you doing here?" Percy asked, pulling away, his face slightly pink.

"I couldn't get my brother to visit me," Barb laughed, "so I came back home to annoy him." She laughed. "I wasn't home more than a couple of days when they found another girl at the lake. So, now I am stuck here a bit longer to help."

"Lillian Dove," Bill introduced. "I'd like you to meet my sister, Barb Fitzgerald."

"Oh, sorry, Lillian." Percy forced his eyes away from the woman whose personality had brightened the room. "Barb and I went to high school together."

Barb walked over to me. "But unfortunately, I have no relation to Scott."

She held out her arm to the room. "Welcome to our Gatsby home."

"Our family was far from being rich," he said, reprimanding his sister. He added for my benefit, "Unless you consider their value for the written word as being rich."

He said, "Both our parents and grandparents instilled in us the value of the written word." Then, he grinned over at his sister, "Although my sister has strayed from journalism to writing fiction."

"Journalism is adopting the ways of fiction," Barb countered. "But my brother, the journalist. is not one to use phrases like dramatic, newsworthy, timely, and eye-catching. And the new jargon word that's becoming my favorite, "Newsjacking." She batted him on the shoulder. "And I only majored in journalism. I never had a career like you."

"Newsjacking," Will repeated, shaking his head. "Horrible word."

"I was thinking about heading home this weekend. I have a deadline looming. But I was here six years ago when the August Lake killer struck. And it looks like it is happening all over again. It must be fate."

"You and Lillian'll get along great," Percy told Barb. "I was telling Bill of Lillian's interest in the history of the lake murders.

She turned her eyes from me to Percy. An eyebrow raised.

I answered, understanding. "Percy and I are just friends."

"Huh?" Percy looked from me to Barb. Then, he turned a thousand shades of red. "Ah, we're not...I mean..."

"Well, a friend of Percy's is a friend of mine," Barb exclaimed. She came over and looped her arm around mine. "Come, my dear. You'll want to hear it all from me, not Bill. After all, I was a witness."

CHAPTER TWENTY-ONE

B arb gave me a tour of the house. Then, we came full circle back to the living room to find Percy and Bill still standing where we'd left them. Barb offered to make sandwiches for lunch.

I turned to Percy, expecting him to inform Barb of our plans to go to the DQ for lunch. But Percy's attention wasn't on me. Instead, Barb had Percy's attention as his eyes were glued to her. "Sounds great."

Barb told them she'd call when ready. And signaled for me to follow her into the kitchen. Once we were alone, she said, "Isn't Percy a sweetheart?" She went to the refrigerator and pulled out sandwich makings. "He told you we went to high school together, but he didn't say we used to be girlfriend-boyfriend."

I had taken bread slices out of the bag and lined them to put on the fixings. I was only half listening, wondering how I could bring the conversation back to her being a witness.

Barb said thoughtfully, "We were serious. I thought I'd marry Percy."

That grabbed my attention. "Really?"

She filled a plate with sandwiches, continuing, "But then, his dad died. And, well, I wanted to go to New York. Become a writer. And he? He felt he was the oldest in his family and had to stay in Frytown and help his mom."

I asked, "Did you move to New York?"

Barb laughed. "I got as far as Ames, Iowa State College. Then I met Bruce, and I fell...well, let's not say in love, more like lust. All the girls on campus thought he was a," she placed her fingers up for an air quote, "catch.' And I couldn't believe how he kept looking at me. Me?" She smiled. "Of course, I wasn't this size when I was in college." She spanked her fanny.

Laughed. "He had these big brown bedroom eyes. And he played football, so his body wasn't bad either. How could I pass him up?" She leaned over and whispered, "I'm very competitive. If the other girls wanted him, I had to ensure I got him." She laughed and said sarcastically, "Lucky me!"

"So you stayed in the Des Moines area?"

"Yep. Still there. I have two kids. But no more Bruce. We divorced three years ago. I found out he had a "catcher's" mitt and was playing ball."

"I'm sorry?"

"He cheated on me with anything that could walk." She sighed, "The best thing to happen to me. By the time we separated, the children had become independent and were living their own lives. They have a good relationship with their dad." She grabbed the plate. "Hey, fellas," she yelled. "You better get in here, or Lillian and I will have a feast."

As we carried the sandwiches and iced tea over to the table, she continued, "I knew marrying Bruce was a mistake." She stopped, paused, thoughtful, "Well, maybe not a mistake. What's the saying, "I am who I am because of the total of experiences I've lived?" She laughed. "Okay, maybe a mistake. Because if I had to do it all over again, I would keep what I wanted to do in life in the spotlight instead of who I wanted. Or at least quit thinking if someone wanted me, I'd won the lottery." She chuckled. "Did they even have the lottery back then? Well, I'm done with husbands. Done with kids." She threw her hands above her head in a sign of victory. "Now, ME!"

"What about me?" Bill asked as he and Percy came into the kitchen. "You didn't tell Lillian how old I was, did you?"

"Are you asking if I told her how you're almost old enough to be my dad?"

"Now, hold on," Bill argued.

Percy laughed and slapped Bill on the back. "That's right, old man."

Bill explained. "Barb and I are fourteen years apart. My folks had two kids; when Dad returned from Vietnam, they had two more. I'm the oldest." He sobered. "War. The perfect birth control. At least for those drafted back in the 60s who had to curtail their lives for those who wanted to play war games." He became thoughtful. "What was it Martin Luther King said? 'The Vietnam War is but a symptom of a far deeper malady within the American spirit." He added, "A malady we and the world still haven't cured. I truly believe it's because war is embedded in our human DNA."

"Do you really believe we are born to kill?" I asked.

"I don't know if I can go that far," Bill said. "But science is finding genetic factors linked to psychopathy, and many murderers have an incapacity for empathy."

Barb exclaimed, "Which is what's going to be me if you don't sit down and start eating. I am starving."

We sat at the breakfast table. Bill and I listened to Barb and Percy exchange friends' names and catch up. I thought they wouldn't move on from the topic until they completed the entire senior roster. I was glad Percy was enjoying himself, but I wanted to discuss the past lake killings.

Percy told Barb, "I didn't hear you were in town, and I swear you would have come and gone if I hadn't brought Lillian over to meet Bill. Guess our coming isn't a coincidence." He smiled big.

I couldn't believe how he was flirting with Barb. Was there still chemistry between the two?

Bill asked me, "How much have you already heard about August Lake?"

"I've Googled a little," I told him. "They had a suspect, right?"

"And let him go," Barb interjected. "DeWade Carruthers. I saw him with one girl in his car just two days before they found her in the lake." She said it as if it were fact, "I know he did it."

Bill picked up. "The police had only circumstantial evidence. Witnesses like Barb said she saw him with one victim."

"Do you know what other evidence they had?" I probed.

Percy said, "Lillian's an investigator. And a pretty good one, too. She's helped the police in several cases."

"Really?" Barb placed both elbows on the table, fists on cheeks, giving me her undivided attention.

"Totally by accident." I pushed the praise away.

I'd been called an investigator for the second time in a matter of days.

I clarified. "I am only interested because of something that happened while I was at the police station the other day."

"What?" All three chorused.

Whoops. "Nothing, really. Someone called in saying someone had kidnapped them."

I tried to make nothing of the event. "But, it turns out Randall Carruthers' ex-girlfriend was out to get him in trouble with the police. No kidnapping."

Barb turned to Bill. "Interesting. Very interesting." Then she said to me, "Before or after they found the girl in the lake?"

If Charles or Leveque heard about this conversation, I'd be dead.

"Charles told me the girl had been in the lake before the girl called the station."

Barb said to Percy, "She purrs when she says Chief Kaefring's name."

"I do not," I exclaimed.

"They've been dating," Percy informed her.

"Were dating," I imparted. "We aren't seeing each other anymore."

"Lucky you," Barb said to Percy.

I had to get the conversation away from me. Bill did it for me. "While the media may connect the past with the present, the medical examiner still holds the death as suspicious."

"Was water in her lungs?" asked Barb. "They say if water isn't in the victim's lungs, they were dead before being placed in the water."

Bill shook his head. "You've been reading too many crime books."

Bill went on, "From what I understand, just because there isn't water found in the victim's lungs doesn't mean they didn't drown. What I am reporting is what the ME told me: the girl had been in the lake for over twenty-four hours. Water was discovered in her lungs. However, according to the ME, a body submerged in water for a long period will passively fill with water. It's why, until tests come back, the stated time of death is hard to calculate."

"Well, I hope they keep an eye on DeWade Carruthers," Barb said flatly. Then, giving me an expression of certainty, "I know he killed those other girls."

Bill reminded Barb, "Remember, you weren't the only witness. Another person came forward, having seen one victim with another man they'd seen down by the lake."

"Is that why they had to let DeWade Carruthers go?" I asked.

"One of the reasons," Bill confirmed. "Also, they found no forensics to link him."

"It has to be Carruthers," Barb insisted.

"And the other missing girl?" I asked.

"Never found," Barb said quietly.

CHAPTER TWENTY-TWO

On the way back to Discount, Percy told me about his and Barb's relationship and how he had to make tough decisions when his Dad died. He could have gone to New York with Barb on her grand adventure or stayed with his mother, whose grief overwhelmed her.

"Mom was a housekeeper. She needed help." He added thoughtfully, not looking at me as he said, "I knew what I might be missing out on by not going with Barb. But sometimes life doesn't always go your way." He then smiled. Said, "Sure, good seeing her again."

We pulled into Discount's parking lot. The store lights were on, and the CLOSED sign now read OPEN.

Hurrying in, I found Dahlia behind the counter.

"What are you doing?"

She leaned her elbows on the counter. "I kept calling here, and no answer. I got worried." She closed one eye and inclined her head. "How will you make a living by closing up during prime-time shopping?"

I almost stammered an answer but caught myself and, in a few steps, I made my way around the counter. "I was having lunch. And it's not prime time. Lunch is slow. I didn't lose any customers. Of course, I was gambling.

She smiled. Big. And I knew I was in trouble.

"Now, I could almost believe that if I hadn't been here myself," she said. "Only I was here, and you weren't. I sold two-fifths of Bourbon, a six-pack of Schlitz, an egg salad sandwich, and a pack of chips. And I've only clocked on for thirty minutes.

I blamed Percy at first, but then I realized it was my fault for not being here.

I answered, "You haven't clocked on. You have to have a job to clock on. And you don't." I said the last words as flatly as I could. Making the don't firm. "How'd you get in here, anyway?"

She hipped herself up on the stool I kept behind the counter. I glanced around but didn't see her walker.

"Told you. I got worried. They found a woman dead in the lake. It could be you next. So, I called the police. Nice officer," she tapped her index finger to her temple, thinking. "Now, what was his name?" She changed her thought. "I talked to someone named Dispatch. She said she was a friend of yours. And when she tried to call your cell, she found I was right. No answer. She offered to send a police officer to the store, but I suggested they pick me up first. I'd be able to let them in and would know if anything was out of order."

"How'd you let them in?"

"With that extra key, you keep in the sugar bowl in the kitchen."

She'd been snooping around.

She said, "I thought I should take the extra key for the house, too. That way, you don't have to worry about me coming and going."

Heat waves radiated off me.

"Which Officer picked you up."

"Nice young man. Newly married, and he told me they're expecting their first."

Office Garth Davis!

"How'd you know what to charge?"

"I didn't at first." She puckered her lips. "Made up what I thought it should cost, and then a customer told me you sell it cheaper. At a discount."

She pointed to the T-shirt she was wearing over her blouse. "I found these in a box back there." She pointed to the storeroom. I brought out a couple to sell." Then she pointed to a small stack of T-shirts. "In various sizes. I told the man buying the Bourbon that if he bought two bottles, I'd give him a free t-shirt." She tapped her head. "Those shirts weren't going to pay for themselves

I hadn't decided what I would do with the T-shirts yet. I'd purchased a few in various sizes and thought I'd figure out a way to get people wearing them.

"Nice man," Dahlia went on. "I wasn't sure what you charged. No price on the bottles, and I couldn't find a price list right off. He told me what he usually pays. I kept it on the loyalty system from there on in." She smiled. "People are honest if you give them half a chance."

I thought that depended on the customer and wondered how much discount she gave the Bourbon. Although giving him a free T-shirt to buy two was a good idea.

Not that I'd tell her. "I'm here now. You're going home."

"You could use my help, Lillian. Instead of closing up when you need to be gone, I could work."

"I have help for that," I countered.

Percy chimed in. "Ah, remember. I only have Wednesdays off now."

I'd forgotten all about Percy and found him standing inside the doorway.

"There, see. What if you need to be gone on other days?" Dahlia rebutted.

"I won't."

She returned, "Well, I guess you do because you weren't here today when I got here. And I handled things just fine."

"Look!" I blasted. "I don't..."

Percy interrupted again. Maybe uncomfortable with the parental confrontation. "If you need a ride home, Mrs. Dove, I can drop you off on my way back into town."

Dahlia slid off the stool. "Thank you. If it's not out of your way."

"Not out of my way at all," Percy smiled.

"Thanks, Percy." I put out my hand to Dahlia. "The key."

She gave me a sideways look. "I'll put it back where I got it."

I wasn't so sure, but what could I do? Besides, Percy was waiting.

Dahlia got her walker out of the storeroom and humped over to Percy. Her t-shirt was still on, making her polyester pants look silly..

Percy picked up the walker in one hand and gave her his arm. "Don't you worry, Mrs. Dove. I've got you."

"Oh, call me Dahlia. All my friends do."

After they'd left, I counted out the cash register. I figured with all that she'd said she'd sold, I would find I was out maybe twenty, fifty dollars. But I was up five. Minus the T-shirt, of course.

CHAPTERTWENTY-THREE

A blue Toyota Corolla was parked in my driveway. When I entered the front door, Dahlia walked out of the kitchen.

"Oh, good. You're on time. I just pulled out the casserole."

I glanced to the living room but saw no one sitting on the couch except for Bacardi.

I whispered, "We got company?" Thinking maybe they had to take a rest in the restroom.

Dahlia shook her head and went back into the kitchen. I followed. The kitchen smelled like heaven. No denying Dahlia could rumble a stomach. Working two jobs, casseroles became her specialty. She made a new one every morning for me to put in the oven for the night's supper.

She placed the dish on a hot pad on the table. The table was set for two.

Still stumped with the *Guess who's coming to dinner"* question, I asked, "Who's car is out there?

She brushed past me. Pulled a tossed salad from the refrigerator. "Mine," she said flatly.

I thought I didn't hear right. "Say again?"

She opened the cupboard and pulled out a Feline Delight can. Bacardi almost knocked me down, getting to his dish.

"Sit down and eat before it gets cold." Dahlia scooped and stirred the Delight into Bacardi's bowl.

"Not until you answer me. Who's car is out in the driveway?"

She turned. Squared her legs to her shoulders. It's mine."

"What do you mean, yours? You can't have a car."

She sat at the table. "Don't see why not. I have a valid driver's license."

"You've had a stroke. It's against the law."

She dished out a scoop of casserole for each of our plates. "Not if you have your doctor's approval. And as soon as my doctor said I was as good as new and could move back to my condo, I went down and renewed my license. I just hadn't got t around to getting a car yet."

"I want to see this license."

She enjoyed her forkful before replying, "Last I knew, you didn't work for the police anymore."

"You can't afford a car. Where did you get the money?"

After she had spent a great deal of her savings when she moved back to her condo with her Oaks Manor boyfriend, Elmer, I suggested I should manage her accounts. Then, if she needed money, all she had to do was ask. I figured, in bringing her to live with me, she wouldn't need much but pocket money.

"Enjoying your dinner, Bud?"

"His name is Bacardi," I reminded her.

"He likes the name Bud," she said. "Don't you, sweet puss."

Bacardi lifted his head from his bowl, gave us each a glance, and then went back to eating. Smart cat.

She took a deep breath and let it out. "What do you want me to do, Lillian? Do you want me to live at Oaks Manor and wait to have another stroke? Maybe this next one will do the trick."

"I..." Of course, I didn't want that. Right?

She continued. "What I have learned the most in life is that I don't get to script it. I am not writing a book moving toward a happy ending. Life is not a happy ending. You die. What comes after is a mystery. Even for those who are really religious."

She said as an aside, "Although there are people who were thought dead and came back alive. They claim they'd seen a light—friends waiting for them. And I don't doubt them. Only I don't want to live my life dying. I want to live it living."

She surprised me. I had never heard her talk like this.

"Each moment is the beginning of my next chapter. And each time I take another step to where I think I want to go, another step reveals itself. And I'm not ready to sign off The End without a fight." She wiggled her empty fork at me. She slid her eyes to mine. "I think your father's main problem was that he liked his addiction and was too afraid of what the day might bring. Especially when he lost his job and couldn't find another one."

She pointed her fork at me. "Sit down before it gets cold." Dahlia patted her head. "You know, I've been thinking about dying my hair again. I dyed it red because I read in a magazine that you must make a bold statement if you want to change things. But the color's wearing on me." She gave her head another pat. "Maybe I'll try for my natural color if I can remember what color that was. Or maybe dye it bluish-grey like rich women in magazines. Helen Miren wore hers in that color. Looked good on her."

I sat in my chair.

I envied what she was saying. I think she meant she could decide her next steps, but she also had to take the following steps that came to her from taking the first. Now she wanted more.

But, then, too, I wasn't sure all this philosophy wasn't a ruse to get me away from what was parked out in the drive.

I asked, "Where did you get the money to buy the car?"

She continued to eat. "Well, when you asked for my checkbook, like you said, on account of you wanting to watch out for me, I pocketed a couple of checks from the back of the checkbook where you wouldn't notice the missing number." She smiled. "Just for emergencies."

"A car isn't an emergency."

"How else am I going to get to the store to help out? I can't ask that nice officer to take me all the time. He has more important things to do than taxi me around."

"I don't want you at the store."

"Don't see why not. I've got experience. I probably know more about running a store than you do."

"What experience do you have?"

"I worked at a store like Casey's when your dad and I were first married to make a little extra money." She must have seen my skepticism. "I had a life before you were born, Lillian."

The comment gave me a moment's thought. I never saw Dahlia beyond the task of taking care of my father, the boys, and me. But, she had been a young child once. She had been a teenager hoping a boy would ask her to the dance. She probably sat contemplating what life would give her or what she had to give back. Then, she fell in love with my father.

"Want to know a secret, Lillian?"

I wasn't sure I did. This was a strange evening, and for some reason, I worried tonight might be just the start of things changing.

I hate change. Taking steps gets me in trouble.

Dahlia said, "You weren't the only one who about killed me. Patrick left home at sixteen. And I knew Frank wanted to leave. But he stayed to help me take care of your father. Your father's drinking got real bad..." she paused, needing a moment, her eyes watering... "especially after you left. You were special to him."

I had to look down at my plate, unable to face her pain. Afraid to have her see mine.

"I guess being the last one home," she continued, "Frank felt responsible. I told him to go on as you two did. But he got a job at the window factory along with me. Said he was destined to stay where he was."

She became quiet. Ate a couple of bites. Maybe she was waiting for me to respond, only I wasn't sure my saying I was sorry would fix the past I'd left for her and Frank.

She got her emotions under control. Her tone was less tired. "I never thought Patrick would leave so soon. But he missed you. And he and Frank didn't get along anymore." She ate another bite and said, "And he said he couldn't sit by and watch his father kill himself."

I understood now how my father committed suicide by slow death. I knew because I had been doing the same.

I wanted to make her feel better. Explain to her that my father had an illness. That he didn't know there was help out there for him.

Like I found for me.

Dahlia set her fork down. "I did everything I could to make your dad happy, Lillian. And each time I told him how worried I was about his health, he'd say, 'You're the best thing that ever happened to me, Dally. But, unfortunately, you can't fix me. I was broke long before I met you."

"What did he mean, broke before you met him?"

She shrugged. "I'm not sure. He wouldn't talk about it. I think maybe he had it bad at home. When he asked me to marry him, it was his way out. Just like he was my way out of leaving and growing up. Girls couldn't just move out on their own back then. We had to be married." She frowned. "You met Pike. I wasn't dating the right kind of guy until I met your father."

Edgar Pike came to Frytown to try to collect his illegitimate inheritance. And when that didn't work, he thought killing his half-sister would get it for him. I stopped him. And if I hadn't, he would have killed his old sweetheart Dahlia, too."

"Why haven't you ever told me any of this until now?"

She looked at me, eyebrow raised. "You never asked. Until you came to Frytown, honey, you weren't much interested in what was happening at home. You couldn't see beyond you."

All you think about is you...it's what I would retort to her when she wanted me to do something that I didn't want to do. When I'd skip school, be gone all day, and not come home until late at night. Drunk more often than sober.

The conversation had gotten away from me. I tried to bring it back to matters at hand. "Still, I don't need your help at the store. And you don't want to get sick again, do you?"

"I've got to do something to make myself useful. I can't sit around looking at that boob tube all day. Or sit petting that cat."

At that, Bacardi yowled. His bowl was empty.

I still wasn't ready to relent. "Who sold you the car? And how do you know you weren't robbed blind? What if you break down? Who's going to help you then? Not me."

The first year I had my vintage Mustang, I always broke down at the most inopportune times.

She huffed. Grabbed the salad bowl and heaped a pile of salad on her plate. "I purchased it from a very reliable dealer, Eddie's Used Cars. And Percy said it was a good car. He said he would advise his own mother to buy it. All I would need to do is change the oil about every three thousand miles. Other than that, he said a Toyota will be running when the world ends." She forked some salad. "That man is sure nice. And he's single."

Damn, Percy. I needed to talk to him. I couldn't believe he went with my mother to buy a car without bothering to call me and talk to me about it.

I had more to say on the matter, but a blast of sirens interrupted our conversation.

"Bet we can beat them," Dahlia challenged.

She was referring to when I was a little kid. When there was a fire, the sirens in town blew to call in the volunteers. Dahlia would stop whatever she was doing and cry out, "Bet we can beat them." We'd run for the car, and she would motor up. "Which way, Lilly?"

"Smoke over there, Mama," I'd point.

Off we'd go, through red lights and stop signs as if we were first responders. More times than naught, Dahlia and I got to the fire, or whatever the situation was, before the New Liberty Fire Department.

A sweet memory.

"We'll talk about this when we get back," I said, jumping up from my chair and looking for my car keys.

"You driving?" Dahlia asked, grabbing her walker where she'd stashed it in the corner of the kitchen. She was using it less and less.

"Well, I'm not getting in a car with you behind the wheel."

We followed the sirens—a howl of pain.

"The lake," Dahlia said, lowering her window and sticking her head out. "They're south of us."

The camping area was full of flaring red and blue lights when we got to Lakeside Drive. And there, in plain sight, a banana-yellow Corvette.

CHAPTER TWENTY-FOUR

Leveque was talking on his phone. Uniform officers were already walking in a zig-zag pattern, looking for anything out of the normal.

"Another girl," Dahlia stated

Hurt me...

The voice was back.

I don't believe in ghosts, but my guilty conscience was definitely haunting me.

Quit it, I told my head.

Help me!

"I can't."

"You can't what?" Dahlia asked, "Are you going to go see what's going on?"

"No."

"Well, I am."

Dahlia got out of the car. She opened the back door and dragged out her walker.

"Dahlia, get back in here."

If Leveque caught sight of Dahlia, he'd start looking for me. And how could he miss seeing an older woman with flaming red hair thumping her walker, making her way over to the crowd gathered outside the police tape?

I watched as Dahlia tried to make her way through the crowd. Then, like parting the red sea, she raised her arms, said something, and thumped all the way to the security tape.

After a few minutes, she looked in my direction and nodded.

Another body.

I watched as Leveque managed the scene. Saw him meet up with the ME.

Dahlia opened the door. "It's another girl," she panted, having hurried.

"Put your walker back in the car. I need to get out of here." At any moment, I was expecting Leveque to zero in on me like a hungry bird after a bug.

Dahlia shook her head. "I ain't ready to go home yet."

"Well, I am."

She fumed, "I should have brought my car. Go on if you want. I'll find a ride home."

A bang shocked the air. Both of us ducked.

"Car backfiring. Go home," Dahlia demanded.

Which put me in a pickle. "Get in," I ordered. I said, "Let's go to the other side where we won't be seen," and then I drove the car. "We'll stay until the ambulance departs. This may be an accident. It might have nothing to do with the other girl they found."

Besides, what started as a lark, replaying a fun moment from the past, had turned out to be someone else's tragedy. But hadn't it always been that way? If sirens announced something fun, would we have jumped in the car so readily? Why are we so moved toward the dark life has to offer?

I kept an eye on Leveque while I waited for Dahlia to get her walker back into the car. The ME and Leveque stood together. The men with the gurney came forward. The ME was shaking his head. Leveque was too, and then, as if angry, he began pacing one way and then another. He said something more to the ME and then got on his phone again.

Who was he calling? Where was Charles?

Bill Egerman stood not far away from the police activity, taking photos. He would call in this latest discovery to the *Iowa City Press*.

I started the car.

As I moved off, I glanced at the crowd. So many of the faces were customers of mine. I figured I'd learn a lotto find out more tomorrow at Discount.

Then, I saw a face I recognized but not one I'd seen at Discount.

It was from a photo on the computer when I was researching. It had been fuzzy, details hard to ascertain. But, as a cruiser moved across the campground, its headlights glaring, it lit a face in the shadows. I immediately had a name.

DeWade Carruthers.

I wondered if Leveque also spotted him.

CHAPTER TWENTY-FIVE

When we returned home, Dahlia immediately turned on the television. But as it turned out, we were ahead of the news. Frustrated with the lack of further information, she said, "Why don't you call and find out what happened?"

"Like who?"

"Call one of your police friends," she suggested, getting excited at the idea of my calling. "You probably know everyone that was there."

Not that I didn't want to. But if I gave Leveque one hint that I was there and that I was attempting to find out what happened, he'd find ways of putting me on house arrest.

Okay, logically, I knew he couldn't do that. I knew Charles wouldn't let him. And Charles wouldn't be vengeful no matter what I had said at Discount. But with Leveque biting at my heels all the time, seeking me out, watching me, jail might not be so bad.

I told Dahlia, "My friends wouldn't tell me anything. No more than they would tell you."

"Maybe I should call that nice officer who gave me the ride."

"No."

But there was someone I could call.

"Sorry to bother you," I said to Barb when she answered the phone. "Has Bill got home yet?"

"He went to the office. Are you calling about the body they found?"

I hadn't seen Barb. "Were you there, too?"

She said, "I went with Bill. They found another girl. But Bill said the situation wasn't the same."

"How?"

"They found this girl half out of the water. And Bill said that this time, there was no doubt it was a homicide."

I thought of seeing DeWade Carruthers watching the activities from the cover of trees. "Do you really think Carruthers is killing these girls?"

"Only one suspect was in the police's custody when they found the last girls. And what goes around comes around." She paused and then said, "They'd better catch him before more girls lose their lives."

CHAPTER TWENTY-SIX

*H*elp!

My lungs hurt. My arms were heavy and tired. Floundering, I desperately tried to keep my head above water. Until I just couldn't any longer.

Water filled my mouth. Choked my throat. And with my watery breath came relief. My lungs eased. My eyes closed. Now, finally, *now I lay me down to sleep.* I waited for the white light. The friends who would greet me. My body sank further and further. Panic didn't overcome me. I was strangely at ease. Is this what death feels like? Just another moment?

And then I saw her. She was lying on the bottom. The muddy water swirled around her as she struggled.

Help!

I liked how I was feeling. No worries. No hurt.

Help me!

Her plea woke me. I started swimming toward her. I was breathing in water as if I had gills. And as I came upon her, I saw the horror of death. What I had been feeling were only its first moments—the first release. Only half-buried bones remained in the mud. Her head was a grayed skeleton. Teeth exposed.

Something, a crayfish, swam out of her mouth.

I stared into the horror of death.

Help them.

CHAPTER TWENTY-SEVEN
THURSDAY, FEBRUARY 12TH

I woke from the nightmare, afraid to fall asleep again. Why was I having these dreams? And what was I supposed to do in having them?

What I did was get up and get dressed. Then, I drove over to the Carruthers' house, where I sat, staring, unsure what I expected of DeWade Carruthers or what I expected of myself.

Was he responsible for these new killings? What had triggered him after having stopped for so many years?

And why was I so compelled to find the answers to these questions?

Save them

The words from my dream echoed.

Shivering, this morning seemed colder than the last. The temperature was dropping. I turned on the car's heater, which seemed only to blow cold.

The Carruthers' house was dark.

Two cars were parked in the driveway. One was the car Randall had been driving. I figured the other one was his father's.

Had Randall told his father that the police had brought him to the station? Accused him of kidnapping the girl who had called dispatch?

I thought back to my breakfast at Connelly's. Randall told Leveque he and Janice went camping on Friday night after work. But that was a lie. According to Janice, she stayed in Frytown. Worked a couple of hours the following day. Why had Randall lied? And why did he want Janice to lie when Leveque talked to her? Randall could have driven back Friday night. Why had he told Janice he was at the campground when he wasn't?

And was DeWade Carruthers really at a conference in Des Moines?

I was burning to let Leveque know about my overhearing Janice. If what I heard was true, Randall could have kidnapped the girl who called the station. But that didn't seem right either. The girl called in and said she lied. The event had nothing to do with what was happening at the lake. And why would Randall have done something that would bring the police right back to looking at his dad again? Although, I don't think Leveque ever really took his eyes off DeWade Carruthers.

I stayed until time to go to work. Back at Discount, customers came in wanting to talk about the recent death at August Lake. Nervous. Anxious. Scared. I didn't discourage them. Several said the August Lake Killer had come back. Some said they thought the killer still lived in Frytown.

After four in the afternoon, Percy came in. He got a Coke out of the cooler and grabbed a bag of chips. He kept looking over at me, and when our eyes met, he'd twist his eyes away. Finally, he brought the merchandise over to the counter. "I was having lunch at the DQ and saw your mother."

Great. Dahlia was driving around town.

Percy asked, "How did you like your mother's car?"

"I didn't."

Okay, a bit sharp. Percy was nice in going with her to find a car, making sure she didn't get duped. But I thought he would have called and talked to me about it first. Apparently, he hadn't expected my answer.

"I asked if maybe she should wait until you were off work." His eyes wouldn't hold to mine. "Bring you with her. But she said you knew noth-ing about cars." He asked for forgiveness, "And I mad,e sure she got a good car for her money. I checked it out good."

I had to relent. Dahlia's car was not Percy's fault. If Dahlia wanted a car that badly, she would have taken a taxi down to the used car dealer.

"I know you did, Percy," I soothed. "But she's had two minor strokes. And she's getting older. She shouldn't be driving anymore."

"Protecting her. I get it." He said, "I stayed and lived with my mom instead of going to New York with Barb. I kept living here in town, telling everyone my mom needed me. He said, "I couldn't think of leaving Frytown while she was alive." He paused, then said, "But that was just what I was saying to myself. My mother didn't need me. She was still putting out a garden every year. Cooking for me up to a month before she passed." His eyes clouded with emotion. "And she's gone, and I haven't left, Lillian. I think it comes down to the fact that I really didn't want to leave. Maybe I was afraid of being out there where I didn't know anyone. What do they call it, out of my comfort zone?"

He said, "I don't think you have to worry too much. Your mom told me she didn't want a car for driving beyond Frytown. Just something to get her from here to there."

If true, what was she doing at the DQ?

"And our city has a lot of seniors like her."

He was right. The town was full of older drivers who couldn't turn their stiff necks to see when they pulled out of a parking place. Who drove ten miles an hour in a thirty zone. Or slowed down at every corner, whether or not a stop sign, as if unsure, a bit lost.

Most of them only drove to the grocery store and back. A doctor's appointment in town. To their grandson's football game at the high school. Even I recognized these drivers and kept an eye out for them.

Percy said, "She mentioned she would visit a friend at Oaks Manor after lunch and then head home unless you needed her help at the store."

I changed the subject. Let Percy out of the doghouse. "I won't be busy until tomorrow and, of course, Saturday."

He grinned. "Glad I got me a date for Valentine's."

I thought he was thinking of me again. But, before I could tell him I'd be too tired to celebrate, he said, "Barb and I are going to dinner at Louise's. Catch up on old times."

Surprised? Yes. But happy for Percy? Absolutely. "You could still get reservations at Louise's?"

He nodded. "The owner of Louise's was a good friend of my mom's. She found a table for us. A little later than the dinner hour, but most people around here like to keep it to around six-thirty. So we've got a reservation for after that."

He asked, "Heard anything more about the girl they found last night?"

I shook my head. "Nothing everyone else hasn't heard."

He gathered his items. "August Lake was the subject of discussion at work. Some say the person who did it is probably the same as last time." He seemed puzzled. "A friend of DeWade's said people could check him off the list. He knows for a fact that DeWade was up in Des Moines at a conference and didn't get back until Monday."

I wondered how the person who said this knew it as a fact.

CHAPTER TWENTY-EIGHT

After Percy left, I enjoyed a cup of coffee, thinking how happy I was for him reconnecting with Barb.

The phone rang. Donna. "Hi, hon. I just wanted to give you a heads up that I may have to take a rain check on my birthday dinner."

"Oh, no. Why?"

"Lieutenant Manville has asked me to do double shifts for the next few days. The third shift is out with a sick kid. And with the Chief away…"

"Where's the Chief?"

"He had to go up North. His wife is sick." She added. "It's not like him to be gone, especially while all this is happening. But I guess she's pretty bad." She answered my how-bad question without my asking. "Critical is what Lieutenant Manville said."

"I hope they find the person who's doing this," I said, hoping she might give me some inside information.

"Detective Leveque told Lieutenant Manville he had a lead he was following. Something from last night's crime scene." She sighed, "Those poor girls."

Then she excused herself from taking another dispatch call. We agreed to schedule another date.

I turned the store sign to CLOSED and left. I headed downtown but reminded myself to stay away from the lake. Passing Oaks Manor, I spotted Dahlia's car in the parking lot. A protective apprehension came over me, like the parent of a teenager who just got their license. Funny how roles reverse.

Then I continued until I came where I knew I shouldn't be.

A forensic team seemed to be still canvassing the area. I parked where I wouldn't necessarily be noticed and stared over to the spot where I thought I'd seen DeWade Carruthers. Again, I wondered if Leveque had also spotted him. And if the lead he'd found, per Donna, set him on Carruthers' trail again.

That made me wonder if Leveque could handle this large case without Charles. Lieutenant Manville was in charge, of course. But Lieutenant Manville was more of a management type, not enforcement.

Quit it. I scolded myself. You're not involved in this. In fact, why was I even here? I should be home watching the boob tube, as Dahlia called it, along with every other Joe citizen.

If I didn't learn to stay away from the police business and concentrate on my goals of creating a life for myself, I would never live with a vengeance. Take it on and show everyone how I could make something of myself.

I didn't believe in Dahlia's philosophy of moments. There was only one big moment, *LIFE*, and you either did it right or wrong.

Angrily, I pulled away from the curb.

A car honked.

I slammed on the brake.

I'd come inches from getting sideswiped.

The driver stopped and gave me a prominent finger wave.

Randall Carruthers.

And someone sitting in the passenger seat. Not Janice.

CHAPTER TWENTY- NINE

T he Mustang's side mirror reflected lights.

A patrol car pulled up next to me, and Officer Garth Davis got out.

"You okay, Lillian?"

"I didn't see him in my mirrors," I quickly explained, thinking he'd witnessed the near mishap.

"The guy was going too fast. He came around the corner, and by the time you looked and went to turn out, he passed. I would have stopped him for speeding, but in this instance, I'm afraid you were in the wrong."

He said, "Can I see your license and registration, please."

"Are you going to give me a ticket?"

"No. No damage was done. We'll make this a warning." He asked, "Where are you headed?"

"Home."

A car horn beeped. Both Officer Davis and I looked over. It was a blue car with an elderly driver with red hair.

I grunted in dismay. I leaned over, opening my cubby to get my registration. Saw the two Snickers bars.

"Let's just make this a verbal warning," Officer Davis said. We heard a voice squawk from his radio. "Stay safe." He hurried back to his patrol car.

I grab Snickers.

I hardly got into the house when I heard, "Careful, too many tickets and your insurance will be sky high." Dahlia chuckling.

"I didn't get a ticket." I headed to the kitchen instead of going into the living room, where I knew she was waiting to raze me.

She shouted, "Looked to me like you were."

"Well, not everything is what it looks like," I countered.

"Police pulling over someone driving a car usually means…"

This subject of conversation needed to spin around back to her. I walked into the living room. "Where have you been?" The question came out more as an accusation than a question.

"I went to see Aurelia. You know, that young man she likes, her assistant? He must have passed his nurse's license. He's her private nurse…"

I was only half listening. A knock at the door ended both our conversations.

Opening it, I found Leveque standing outside.

Wonderful. This day was just getting better and better. "What are you doing here?" I growled.

He countered, "Who's car is in the driveway?"

"None of your business."

From behind me came Dahlia's voice. "It's my car."

Leveque squeezed himself past me. "Nice."

"Runs like a beaut," Dahlia said.

He came back to where I stood. Where I pointed, demonstrating the way out.

He ignored me. "Garth said you were in an accident on Lakeside."

"I didn't reply."

"Accident?" echoed from inside.

I lowered my voice. "First, I didn't have an accident. And second, if it is any of your business, and it's not, I was at Louise's."

I figured Officer Davis may have mentioned seeing me. He may even have shared with someone I had a near accident. And that someone could have been Leveque. But I was reasonably sure Officer Davis did not mention my exact location.. And businesses make up Lakeside Drive before the street parallels August Lake.

"Then you admit to being there." Leveque raised his chest in a huff. Scowled.

Smug.

I calmed myself. Then, I took hold of the door and began to shut it on him. "As I said, I wasn't expecting company. And we were just about to sit down to dinner."

"What are we having?" I whipped around to find Dahlia standing behind me. She was holding Bacardi. They both purred. "Something from Louise's?" Dahlia cooed.

She damn well knew we weren't.

"Why don't you go on in and put dinner on the table," I highly suggested.

I put a hand on Leveque's shoulder and pushed. "Thanks for the surveillance and for noticing the additional car in our drive. But we are fine, thank you."

"Why don't you stay for dinner?" Dahlia invited.

"Thanks for the invite." He called over my shoulder. "Maybe another time." Then, he took ahold of my arm. And pulled.

He caught me unaware. I stumbled out the door.

"Take your hands off me."

Leveque closed the door and stood in front of it. "I'm going to make this short, but not sweet."

I stepped to shove past him. But, unfortunately, he was stronger than me.

"With the Chief gone, I'm in charge of this investigation. And I will NOT have you meddling."

"Parked in front of a restaurant is not meddling."

"I could access your exact location by cameras, but to be frank, I don't have the time. If you don't quit, you may cause someone else to get hurt."

A veiled threat. Nothing I had done so far would have escalated whoever was murdering these women.

I wasn't sure what his next move might be. Leveque has put me in handcuffs before to make a point.

I stood without a coat, but I wasn't cold. Not then. A boiling heat steamed off me from his audacity in trying to control me. I abruptly changed the subject. "How is Charles' wife?"

His eyebrows raised. Dimples popped. "Isn't the Chief keeping you appraised of his domestic problems?"

His overall arrogance was appalling. And I would not respond. By not responding, it proved his remark had no effect. I hadn't heard from Charles since finding him at Discount waiting for me. "I'm sure Charles would enjoy hearing you referred to her illness as a..." distinct pause, domestic problem."

Leveque might be physically stronger than me, but I was done with this interrogation. "So, Garth Davis told you about an incident down on Lakeside? Did he tell you the incident occurred because Randall Carruthers was driving like a bat of out of openedhell?"

He started to open his mouth.

"Did you know Randall also has another friend that's a girl? I wonder if Janice knows."

"And, did Janice mention to you how she and Randall didn't go to Carrollton on Friday night like planned?"

Every muscle in his face, even his dimples, clenched. "Where'd you hear that?"

If he had given it a second thought, he'd have remembered me coming out of Connelly's. But he was still stinging from my one-two punch.

"Did she tell you she couldn't leave until Saturday morning?"

The eyes don't lie. Leveque's wavered, quickly processing.

He hadn't known.

He punted. "Carrollton's camp registration shows Carruthers checked in at six -fifty-eight, Friday evening."

"That is pretty weak, Leveque. If I had said that to you, you would have told me there wasn't any reason for Randall to notify anyone of his leaving again.

He steeled me a look. I smiled. "It's only a two-hour drive."

His lids lowered. The steeled look was still piercing. I was enjoying the stabs on his ego. I enjoyed it so much that I could have done a happy dance right then and there.

A happy dance would have warmed me up.

Turning the tables again, I threw what I had left at him. "Did DeWade's alibi pan out? Why was this second girl found partially out of the water? Was the job botched, or did he intentionally place her there for quick discovery??"

I reached out and took his arm. Pulled him away from the door. "On your watch, Leveque. Two women dead. No suspects."

At first, he resisted. But, as I pulled, he came close. So close, the muskiness of his anger was confusing.

His breath hotly teased my neck. "I want you to stay away from all of this. You think you have it all figured out, but you're wrong, Lillian. And if you don't stay away, you will get hurt."

I pulled back. Whispered slowly, "If I hear of anything else that might be helpful, I'll let you know." Then said as if I meant it, and I did, "And don't worry about me, Leveque. I can take care of myself."

Before he could stop me, I opened the door and slammed it closed. Inside the house, Dahlia stood facing me.

"He's very handsome, isn't he?"

Outside, a squeal of tires.

CHAPTER THIRTY

The supper was simple—egg scramble. I led the conversation to Oaks Manor, wanting to keep Dahlia away from anything she might have overheard. And I was sure she'd had her ear to the door. "How was Mrs. Goyen?"

"Aurelia didn't look well. I think she's getting worse."

Again, I could have mentioned Nelly's opinion on Mrs. Goyen's health, but I let it go. "You said she has a private nurse now?"

"Well, as well as one. It's the young man we met in her room. She said he brings her lunch or dinner from restaurants when visiting. They seem to get along well. And this time, he didn't leave during my visit." She picked up some scramble with her fork. Leaned her head coyly. "But who wouldn't like a young man around?" Her fork wagged. "This Officer Leveque. He's about your age, isn't he? Is he married?"

I wasn't going there. "Why were you so enamored with Mr. Goyen?"

Dahlia's eyes widened. She set down her fork. "I told you, there was nothing between Bernie and me. He was a lonely man. When Aurelia fell asleep, we'd watch television together."

"Lonely?" I giggled with my inside joke, "Not by a long shot."

She startled. "Maybe you don't understand the toll of caring for someone sick. Even if you have help, as Aurelia does, it feels like you're alone. You feel like life turned on you, and instead of bringing...."

"Well," I giggled. "Bernie Goyen was far from being alone." I couldn't help it. The giggles were bubbling up inside me like a seltzer.

"Don't you dare insinuate..."

"You weren't the only one Bernie was...air quote...' "watching television with.' When I went to Pella, I found another Mrs. Goyen."

She sputtered. "What are you saying?"

"Bernie Goyen was a bigamist."

"I don't believe you."

I shrugged. "Believe me or not. It doesn't matter anymore. He's dead. And Bette Day is known in Pella as Bette Goyen. The neighbor also knew Bernie. She commented on how his job caused him to travel a lot."

Dahlia slumped in her chair from the shock of what I was saying. I should have stopped. But I couldn't. The seltzer had been shaken.

"And I met Bernie's son. Bernie Junior. He told me he'd severed ties with his father years ago. I bet he found out about his father's first wife...the one he was still married to."

"I can't believe this."

"Believe or don't." I got up from the table. Put my plate in the sink.

"You can't tell Aurelia," Dahlia said. "This would kill her."

I snipped, "I thought she was already dying?"

I left her sitting at the table, grabbed my coat, and slammed the front door. It wasn't one of my finer moments. And it wasn't Dahlia that had gotten under my skin. It was Leveque.

CHAPTER THIRTY-ONE

While I may have surprised Leveque with the information I knew, I hadn't asked him any question I had no answers for. Only what if DeWade had been at the conference and his alibi checked out? Who would Leveque suspect next? What new lead did he have?

I thought back to Mrs. Goyen, saying Dahlia told her I was a good investigator. How had she put it? *Your mother's always telling everyone how good you are at finding out things.* And hadn't Percy said I had a knack for *ferreting out vermin*? I remember telling him it was more like vermin seemed to seek me out.

Was that true?

Thinking back to Sunday morning, I couldn't see how any choices I made tossed me into the ring with Leveque yet again. Did this mean my destiny was putting me in these situations? Or was I always making bad choices? How did I know which? What is fate? An act of compulsion? I had visited Dispatch at the exact moment the girl called, saying someone had kidnapped her. If I had taken longer when talking to Nelly at Oaks Manor or called Donna instead of visiting her at the station, Donna would have taken the call.

Was I moving by choice where I was to go next? Or were the winds of fate taking me? Maybe life moments are like the big bang. We are born with the experiences we have, and we are moving toward them throughout our lives.

Because I hadn't made good decisions until I came to live in Frytown. But, when I moved here and pulled myself away from my old life, I vowed to take on a new me. And I think I'm headed in that direction. I am sober. I am living my life differently. But does living life differently mean living it the way I see others living their lives? Or should I follow life where it takes me?

I hate having more questions than answers. And no one I could ask. All these thoughts were giving me a headache.

Then, my phone rang.

CHAPTER THIRTY-TWO

"**O**kay, I'll bite. If it wasn't Janice Roberts, who was it?"

I could have baited Leveque by pretending to withhold a name. But I knew how much it took for him to call me.

"I don't know," I said truthfully. "I didn't get a good look at her. The girl was about his age, small in the passenger seat compared to Randall. Brown hair, in a bobbed style."

"Bob?"

"Styled like a bubble around her head."

"Nola Cross."

The name surprised me. We stayed quiet, giving that some thought. Finally, he said, "Which gives me two questions."

I made a guess. "My first question is why did she call Dispatch unless it was like Charles said—a girlfriend's act of vengeance?"

"And the second question would be," Leveque added, "Why is she driving around town with who she said kidnapped her?"

"Maybe he grabbed her again," I weakly guessed.

"Or the two of them are playing a game."

"And Randall's dad's alibi?" I tendered. "He could have done it if he wasn't at the conference like he said."

"His alibi stands," Leveque said. "Those at the conference validated his attendance. Including his partner, who was there with him. They didn't check out until Monday morning and came back together." He added,

"That's all I am telling you, Lillian. And I'm not sure why I told you that much. I don't want you getting involved."

So, what Percy heard was true. I thought back to seeing DeWade across from the station while Leveque was questioning Randall. Should I tell Leveque? I said, "I think it's too late for my getting involved, Leveque. Regardless of whether I want to be, something is pulling me. I was at Dispatch just as that call came in. I saw DeWade Carruthers outside the police station when I left on Monday."

"What time Monday? And how do you know it was DeWade?"

"I didn't, not then. But when I checked about the past crimes at August Lake on Google, I saw a photo of him."

"Just curious," Leveque quipped.

"I am glad I am, or I wouldn't have recognized him when they found the second girl."

"Lillian, you think you've pulled some pieces of this case together? But you haven't. Not all is as it seems." But, then, what I'd said must have zeroed into his brain. "What do you mean you recognized him when the second girl was found?"

I told him, "He was there. I saw him."

Leveque was quiet for a moment or two, but then his voice rose, loud and angry. "Stay away, or you're going to get hurt. And I don't have time to protect you while building a case to stop a madman."

A buzzing tone filled my ear. He'd hung up.

I guess he hadn't seen DeWade at the lake. And what did he mean that Randall and Nola were playing a game?

I wondered then if I was, like Leveque said, pulling pieces together and forcing them to fit.

One thing I knew, I was suddenly hungry for a DQ cheeseburger.

CHAPTER THIRTY-THREE

I was in luck. Jamie was at the counter.

The place was almost empty. I checked out the menu, read each description, and then went to the counter where she was waiting to take my order.

"What are you going to have, Lillian?"

"Cheeseburger with everything."

She laughed. "You're usual then."

"When something's good, it's better not to mess with it. I can count on the Cheeseburger."

She punched in my order. "Want fries with that?"

I thought of the now cold scrambled eggs I'd left on the table. "Sure, why not."

Since things were slow, Jamie stayed at the counter to chit-chat.

I looked around, trying to seem nonchalant. "Have you and your friend popped the top on that Pink Vodka yet?"

She grinned. "I've resisted. I want to make Valentine's night special."

Again, I glanced around. "You haven't seen Nola Cross come in tonight, have you?"

"Nola? I don't think so."

"I heard she might be looking for a job," I lied.

"Really? Then she's not going back up to Ames?"

Iowa State College. I maneuvered myself out of one lie and into another. "I heard she was still dating Randall Carruthers, so I thought maybe she wasn't returning."

"Really? Because they broke up at the end of their Senior Year. I think he is dating Janice Roberts now. But what either of them sees in him is beyond me. He's trouble."

Instead of offering another lie, I changed my subject to Randall. "He can't be that bad."

"He's mean and controlling." She leaned toward me. "He asked me out one time. This was before his dad was suspected of killing those girls at the lake." She frowned. "I don't think Mr. Carruthers had anything to do with those girls being murdered. He comes here to the DQ, and people give him a wide birth. But he's always nice to me."

If Jamie were on a jury, a nice defense would carry weight. She did her own glancing around before adding, "Randall would be more the type."

"You orderin' or waitin', sweetheart?"

I turned around. "Sorry. I didn't know you were behind me.

"Don't mind waiting for a good-looking girl like you." He gave me a board, yellow-toothed smile. One front tooth was missing.

I move away from the counter, moving to the side and busying myself with getting napkins and ketchup. I heard him order and begin chatting Jamie up by asking if she had ever visited Maquoketa and its famous bat caves.

While eating, I thought back to what Leveque guessed, that the girl in Randall's car was Nola Cross. So why would Nola be riding around with Randall? And did Janice know that she was?

Leaving DQ, I saw a cruiser. From the shadow inside, I'd swear it was Leveque. So why was he following me? Because he thought I was on the trail of the case? Hoping I would lead him to something? The bat-man's old broken-up truck was parked next to my Mustang in the parking lot.

Full and getting sleepy, I considered going home, but I wasn't ready to go back to the discussion about Mrs. Goyen. So instead, I drove around. I thought about going by Bill Egerman's to see if I could get more information from him. But he would be busy writing up his story for the Gazette, and I didn't want to bother him. It's better not to overuse sources until you need to. Then, of course, I could stop by and see Barb. But just having met her, I didn't really have a good excuse for a sudden visit. Too transparent.

I drove around the streets, knowing where I wanted to go but telling myself I shouldn't. Back at the Carruthers' house, I saw both cars were in the drive. Lights on. The flicker of a television. I also saw a dim light at a ground-level window. The basement? Leveque claimed that Carruthers held the girls there when the first August Lake murders occurred. But Charles had said there wasn't any forensics to prove it.

I thought back to the call I had taken when Nola claimed she was in a basement.

Suddenly, I saw a shadow in one of the front room windows. As if someone heard a motor out by the curb and peeked to see who it was. I drove on. Driving back to the crime scene. The tape was still up, some torn and floating in the wind, but the park was empty of people and police cars. I parked on the street and then walked to the lake. There was enough light from the moon to find my way, and I tried to keep in the shadows.

I didn't feel alone. I could hear voices of people going in or coming out of Lousie's down the street. Cars moved up and down Lakeside, with someone's radio playing Adel's *Easy on Me*. When I came to the edge of the lake where the body had been found, I remembered Barb saying, *Bill said this time there was no doubt it was a homicide.*

Then, I heard something. I let my eyes adjust to dark images and grey shadows. Leveque? I saw no one, but someone was there. I could feel their eyes on me. I then looked to where I had seen DeWade Carruthers. And from out of the shadows, movement.

I tried not to panic. Instead, I began walking causally back to my car. If Leveque wanted another face-off, I was ready for him. He was definitely stalking me.

I turned.

It wasn't Leveque.

It was Randall Carruthers.

I ran.

CHAPTER THIRTY-FOUR

The thump of footfalls behind me told me he was in pursuit.

I grabbed my keys out of my coat pocket. Readied the house key, longest and sharpest, between my knuckled index and middle finger. Aim for the eyes, I reminded myself.

I tripped when stepping over the street's curb. My breath rose in panic. The key loosened. Dropped.

I got up and fell. I'd twisted my ankle.

I checked behind me, thinking that I may have outdistanced him. And if so, maybe he had given up. But he stood no more than twenty feet away. Breathing hard.

I grabbed my phone. I knew there was an icon to call for emergency, but damn if I knew where it was. I put in my security code to open my phone.

He began coming towards me. Slow but steady.

"I've called the police," I yelled, fingering to dial 911.

He stopped. Put his hand up. "Are you hurt?"

Okay, not the question I was expecting.

He was wearing jeans and a black hoody. The hoody covered a dark baseball cap with a red bill and an image of a red devil.

A voice asked, "911. What is your emergency?"

He glanced at my phone and said, "I'll be gone before they get here. Or, you can listen to what I have to say. I'm not here to hurt you."

He could have fooled me. What was he after?

He stated, "My father killed these women."

Why was he telling me this? "Then you should go to the police." I glanced around, wishing for a car to drive by.

Again, the voice from the phone. "Frytown Police. What is your emergency?"

Randall said, "I don't have any proof. That's where you come in."

"Is anyone there?" It was Donna's voice. She was handling the second shift.

I had to decide quickly what I was going to do. While my cell number might not provide the caller-ID, Donna would follow up on the call. The authorities should establish the location of the call and dispatch a patrol. Dispatch got false 911 calls. People who made a mistake dialing, or kids who had nothing better to do than prank public services. Which would cause parents to be fined. But Donna would see that this call came from the August Lake vicinity. She wouldn't dismiss it as a prank.

The sound of a car pulling into the parking lot broke the moment. Both of us turned to look.

Randall said, "I know you're hip-jointed to Detective Leveque. I need you to tell him something for me."

"Don't be a scary cat," someone from the parking area shouted. "Come on."

The voices were kids. Then, "Hey, it's the cops. Let's go." A car door slammed. A motor gunned. Red and blue lights fired from a patrol car turning into the lot.

Feeling safer now that the police were within shouting distance, I asked Randall, "Why don't you tell Detective Leveque?"

He returned, "I'll give you evidence." He took a step forward.

"Don't come any closer. The police are here. They'll hear me if I scream."

"Meet with me. In public. I'll give you evidence my father is a murderer. You can be the town hero again."

BANG!

Randall dropped to the ground.

I covered my head.

But it wasn't a gunshot we'd heard. Instead, an old truck passing by had backfired.

He craned his head around, maybe looking to see if the police were heading our way. I looked, too. Where were they?

He said, "If you want the truth, meet with me." His words rushed. "Or more women will wind up dead." A beam of light passed over us. He turned around to leave.

I heard myself say, "Where?"

He said over his shoulder as he hurried to the street, "Shorty's after you close up the store."

Did he know about the store? I'd never known him to come into Discount. I told him, "It's Friday. I will probably close late."

"I'll wait." And then he was gone.

The flashlight blinded me. Behind it came Sergeant Minor. "Is that you, Lillian?"

"It's me."

"Was it you who called dispatch?"

Should I tell him about Randall? I decided not to. After all, Randall only frightened me. "Yes. I fell and twisted my ankle. It hurt like hell, and I thought I might need an ambulance, but I'm okay." I stood, took a step, squealed with the sharp pain, but took another. "I've just sprained it."

Sergeant Minor came over, helping me by taking my arm. "Are you out here alone? What are you doing here?"

"Like everyone else. I was just curious."

"Hasn't anyone ever told you curiosity killed the cat?"

"They also say a cat has nine lives."

He didn't laugh.

Mitch Miner was a patrol officer when I worked at the FPD, but he made Sergeant after I left. Well over five foot, a bit stocky but wearing the weight well in his uniform, he was a good cop and well-liked by other officers. He and his wife, Sue, did a lot of charity work in town. He was renowned for bringing joy to those in poverty by delivering presents and meals at Christmas.

He searched the area with his flashlight. "You're sure you were alone? I thought I saw someone else."

When Leveque heard Miner found me at the lake, he would be on me like a leach. If I mentioned Randall Carruthers, he'd suck my blood dry.

"Just me," I said. "I was at Louise's. I just stopped here for a minute. Don't know what I was thinking."

He gave me a steadied glare. "We both know what you were thinking."

I raised my hand. "No, really. I raised my hand and said, "I just wanted to see where the girl was killed. Nothing else."

CHAPTER THIRTY-FIVE
FRIDAY, FEBRUARY 13th

T he sky was smeared with grey clouds.

So cold a coat wasn't a consideration but a must.

And I had awakened early. I slept little after returning from August Lake with Randall Carruthers' plea for me to meet him later in the day. And I tried to imagine what he could mean that he had evidence his father was responsible for the killings.

What evidence?

Was it the same lead Leveque was following?

During the interview with Leveque, Randall claimed his father's innocence. So why the change tonight? Was it a son's loyalty over right vs. wrong? Or had something else happened that caused Randall Carruthers to seek me out?

And why me?

When I got to Discount, cars were already in the parking lot. White air exhaust billowed like the smoke from medieval dragons.

My phone rang before I got out of the car.

Dahlia. "Lillian, where did you go?"

"To work."

"I need you to go with me to see Aurelia."

One, I couldn't understand why Dahlia was so besotted by Aurelia Goyen. If she called saying she was dying again to get Dahlia to do something for her, I sure wasn't going to bite.

"You have a car," I reminded her.

"Yes, but what if she asks me about Bernie? What do I tell her?"

"Tell her the truth." I hung up and hurried into the store. Flipped the sign to OPEN—no sense making the early birds wait any longer—hurried back, opened the door, and gave a wave to come in. I clicked on the heat, filled and started the coffee before hearing the first jingle of the door's bell.

Some conversations during the day started and ended with the weather. *I thought winter was done with us. Getting cold enough to snow. The temperature dropped overnight. This cold will kill all the flowers. The groundhog saw its shadow, damn groundhog. Farmer's Almanac predicted an extended winter. I knew better than to store away my snow tires. They say we can get up to two feet of snow.*

But all conversations, too, came around to nervous chatter about the latest August Lake victim. *Another girl was found at the lake. Have you heard the victim's name yet? I'm sure not going out tonight. Heard this time it is one of our girls. I'll stay home where it's safe. Keep mine inside with me. Heard this one's different. Why the hell is Chief Kaefring gone? He'd better get back here. Can't let this guy get away with it again. Which girl?*

It was close to seven by the time I closed the store. I tossed the coin whether to head to Shorty's and doubted I'd find Randall.

I didn't frequent Shorty's, but many in Frytown were loyal customers. A simple, unassuming building on Main Street, it carried a humble sign declaring *Shorty's Good Eats.*

The restaurant had a moderate number of customers. Randall was sitting in the far back of the restaurant. Baseball cap low on his head. Those seated as I walked by kept to their conversations.

Randall's eyes remained on the table as I sat down.

I asked, "What am I doing here?"

Still, he kept his eyes down and his voice low. "Like I told you. I need you to tell Detective Leveque my dad is guilty."

"Why me? Why not tell him yourself?"

He grunted. "Don't like cops. Besides, I heard you helped him with the Dyre drug arrest."

No one knows me if they don't come into Discount, but the drug arrest on the Cartel at Frytown's Dyre Moving Company entered conversations.

"Helped is using the term loosely," I said. "I was there when the police made the arrest, along with the FBI."

"Not what I heard," he returned. "Word is it's not the first time you've shown up the police."

Is that what people were saying? If so, I could understand why Leveque gritted his teeth each time my interest peaked. I said to Randall, "You said you have proof?" Not that I was going to agree to be his intermediary, but, hey, I was at Shorty's. I might as well see what he had.

His head swiveled a one-eighty. Then he said lowly, "He killed my mom."

I don't know what I expected, but that wasn't it.

"Your mom? How do you know?"

"I saw him. I heard them arguing. When I opened their bedroom door, I saw him hit her. Hard. She fell. She was bleeding. He told her to get up, but she didn't. He killed her."

"How old were you?"

"Five. Six."

I could see why this might lead him to think his father was the killer, but was what he was saying true? "Does your father know you think he killed your mother?"

"Oh, yeah. He saw me when he did it. He told me if I didn't want some of the same, I'd better get my tail back to bed."

Witnessing an event like that could leave a lasting impression. "Did you see your mom after that night?"

"I told you he killed her. You aren't listening." He looked up and grilled me with his eyes. "No, I didn't see her again. I didn't see her ever."

I continued, "What about at the funeral?"

He grumbled, "I thought you were smart. There wasn't any funeral. He got rid of the body."

I countered. "Someone had to have noticed she was missing. What did your father tell the police?"

He shrugged. "Not sure the police bothered."

I could understand that if he had seen his parents arguing. If he had seen his father hit his mother. And he didn't see his mother again. He might think she had been killed. "How do you know your mother didn't leave your father?"

His head jerked. His voice raised in volume. "She would NEVER have left me. Maybe him. But, NOT ME."

The voices in Shorty's cut short. I didn't look, but could feel heads turn our way. They may not know me, but they probably knew Randall Carruthers, no matter how low he was wearing his cap.

I remembered Janice Roberts saying that Randall's mother left when he was a baby. But this wasn't exactly evidence. "Is this all you have?"

He glared, "Isn't it enough?"

"No."

"Why not?"

I told him, "I've heard from others—not the police—that your father's alibi held up. He wasn't here."

He returned, "Des Moines isn't more than a couple of hours away. So he could have driven back."

I gave that consideration. "Yes. A two-hour drive isn't much." I added, "But an hour from Carrolton isn't long, either."

His eyelids lowered, face darkened. "Tell Leveque. He's been trying to lock up my dad for years. He'll love this information."

I shook my head. Not because I disagreed with him. First, there was no way I was going to tell Leveque I met with Randall. And second, if I told Leveque my evidence for DeWade Carruthers' arrest was Randall's mom missing, he'd laugh himself silly.

Only Randall took my negative headshaking as a sign I was refusing to do his bidding. He slammed the palms of his hands down on the table. Then, he leaned over at me, spittle striking me as he roared, "I told her you were a waste of time."

Who told him? Janice?

He left abruptly.

Again, conversations halted. This time, heads turned as Randall passed tables. And when he banged the door on his way out, heads twisted around towards me. I shrugged. "I told him I wouldn't pay for his Cheese Burger."

I then got up and ordered. Not exactly DQ's, but good. While I ate, I went over the conversation. And wondered what I should do with what he'd told me. If anything.

Only I didn't need to decide. On the way home, the news reported that the police had just released the name of the latest girl found at August Lake. And it was one of ours. Janice Roberts.

I'd been headed home, but hearing the name, I immediately changed direction.

CHAPTER THIRTY-SIX

J anice Roberts?

I headed straight to Leveque's house. Whether he wanted my help or not, he needed to know about my meeting with Randall. His setting me up to meet with him couldn't have been a coincidence. My head was on a fast track with questions, and I couldn't grab anything that felt logical.

I knew where Leveque lived but wasn't a frequent visitor. The last time I was there, I'd painted a massive sign in the snow in his front yard, making fun of a nickname I was trying to pin on him, Samson.

The house was dark.

I immediately backed out of the driveway and headed to the station. It was the only other place he would be. And knowing Leveque, not able to drop the string leading from one piece of evidence to the next, I should have gone there first.

The Corvette was in the parking lot. He could be out on one of the cruises, but I went in anyway. Dispatch would know where I could find him.

Before I got to the lobby door, I heard the roar of car engines. The parking gate squealed open. I ran. And stood to where Leveque couldn't help but notice me.

He stepped on the brakes. Got out of the car. Yelled, "Are you crazy? I could have hit you."

"We need to talk," I shouted.

Then Sergeant Minor came running out of the back station door. Behind him, Lieutenant Manville.

"Get out of the way, Lillian," Leveque ordered. Now!"

Three cruises drove out. I watched, dumbstruck, and wanted to follow them.

My phone rang.

Dahlia said, "Lillian, Aurelia's missing."

"What do you mean, missing? Nelly will know where she is."

"Nelly said she doesn't know where she is, but she did say Mrs. Goyen went with Michael yesterday and hasn't returned."

"Then she's not missing. She's with him." I looked longingly down the street at the fiery lights of Frytown's finest. "I've got to go, Dahlia."

"Nelly told me Michael's last name. Michael Day. Does that ring a bell for you?"

"Where are you?"

"Home. Where are you?"

"Headed to Oaks Manor."

I glanced at where I wanted to go, then got back in my car to go where my gut told me something wasn't right.

Nelly, and Mary Niles, the night-time shift RN, were at the desk when I walked through the doors. I turned to a frantic Nelly, biting her bottom lip and looking like a mother who had lost one of her children.

"Dahlia called and told me Mrs. Goyen is missing," I said, coming up to the desk.

"Let's not say missing," Mary Niles said. "It implies that we may have lost her."

"Then you haven't lost her? You know where she is?"

Nelly shook her head. Mary glanced beyond me to the front doors as if expecting Mrs. Goyen to return any minute.

I asked, "Have you called the police?" It was a reasonable question since the timeline Dahlia gave me made it at least twenty-four hours of not hearing from their resident.

Mary and Nelly exchanged glances. "I want to," Nelly said.

"It's not like our residents are prisoners here, Nelly." Then, again, Mary offered me the logic she was basing her decision upon. "Mrs. Goyen doesn't suffer from dementia, which would require us to notify the police. And we know who she's with."

Nelly's eyes filled. "They say they found another body at the lake."

"Don't be ridiculous, Nelly," Mary warned. "Michael is not the lake killer." Mary turned to me. "All we know is that Michael told one of the nurses that he was going to treat Mrs. Goyen to an afternoon out for lunch."

"Do your nurses often take residents out?"

"Only in special circumstances," Nelly returned. "But Michael isn't part of our staff. Or a nurse that I am aware of."

Mary said, "Michael started volunteering here. He visits with residents. Reads to some."

I asked, "How long has he been a volunteer?"

She thought before answering. "How long. Nelly? Six. Seven months, maybe?"

I asked Nelly, "After her husband died?"

Nelly nodded. "Not long after Mr. Goyen passed." Nelly said, "He seemed like such a nice young man. He said he wanted to go into nursing. Although, I think he's a musician. He brings his guitar and plays for us."

"What should we do, Lillian?" Mary asked.

"Should we call the police?" Nelly asked.

Micheal came to Oaks to volunteer shortly after Mr. Goyen passed. Was Michael Day Bernie Goyen's grandson? If so, was he seeing Mrs. Goyen because he was angry about his grandfather's bigamy? The deceit to his father? Vengeful for the pain Bernie may have caused his grandmother?

While Michael showed no animosity toward Mrs. Goyen when in her presence, it sure appeared that he'd especially come to Oaks Manor to volunteer to get close to her. And develop a relationship with her to where he became what Mrs. Goyen told Dahlia was her private nurse.

I looked up on my phone the information I'd purchased on Bette Day. I took a shot at calling her before calling the police. She answered by the third ring.

"Bette Day?"

"Yes."

"My name is Lillian Dove. I am calling with a concern for your grandson, Michael."

"Michael? Has something happened?"

"Have you seen him recently?"

"Not recently. He lives in Iowa City, where he works." Her voice grew more concerned, "What has happened?"

"I believe he has taken Aurelia Goyen. They have both been gone since yesterday. Bette, do you have any idea where he may have taken her?"

Her voice escalated from concern to anger. "Aurelia Goyen? What do you mean? Michael has no idea who she is."

"Oh, but he does know. He has been volunteering at Oaks Manor here in Frytown for the last several months. The staff has told me Mrs. Goyen was last seen with Michael. Do you have any idea of where he may have taken her?"

Bette Day demanded my cell number and said she would call me right back.

Nelly and Mary had listened to my conversation. I asked Nelly, "Do you have any idea where he may have taken her?"

"No," Nelly shook her head, biting her bottom lip with worry.

Mary said, "Mrs. Goyen has been saying lately that she might be able to move back home. Michael offered to take care of her."

"Do you have her address?"

Nelly turned and went over to her computer. Started tapping keys.

My phone rang. "Miss Dove. My mother told me you've contacted her." It was Bernie Goyen.

"I am concerned about Mrs. Goyen, Mr. Goyen. She has been missing for twenty-four hours and was last seen with someone who is known here at Oaks Manor as Michael Day. Michael is your son, am I right?"

"Michael wouldn't hurt her." His voice was calm, without surprise or concern.

"You know about his relationship with Aurelia Goyen?"

"No. But Michael was aware of her." He said, "My son was very close to his grandfather. He may have learned of the situation and sought her out. Please do not call the police. I will find him. I will make sure that Aurelia comes back without harm."

"If that doesn't happen within the next few hours, Mr. Goyen, I will have no choice but to get the police involved. Let's hope you're right. That your son has no ill-intent toward your father's legal wife."

I clicked off with him. Turned to Nelly. "Do you have that address?"

She handed it to me.

"If they didn't go to her place, I will have no other choice but to call the police, whether his father calls back or not."

I drove across town.

The address was on Washington Street, which I found ironic. Bernie did tell a lie. The house was a large, historical Victorian. Three stories high which explained why it was hard to care for Mrs. Goyen in the home. Victorians generally have small rooms and stairways.

A large sun porch offered a swing for those relaxing summer nights. A Christmas wreath still hung at the front door. The lights were on in the downstairs rooms, and unless the Goyens rented the house or had sold it since Bernie's death, it hinted someone was home.

I parked a few houses down. It was getting colder. I wrapped my coat tightly around me and tried to ignore the wet splattering. I went up to the front door. The window in the door offered a view of a wooden circular stairway rising to the second floor. A bay window showed a dining room with a large chandelier hanging above a dining room table. Then, I went to the large front window with the lights on. I peeked into the living room. I could see Micheal. He was talking excitedly on his cell phone, hands making motions as if what he was listening to disagreed with him. His father? Then, I saw Mrs. Goyen. She was seated over by a lit fireplace in a club chair with an afghan tucked around her. She was watching Michael closely.

The firelight flickered on her pale skin. Her hair had been combed and pulled tightly away from her face, causing her features to seem stark and sharp.

Michael clicked off his phone, dropping it onto a table by a small sofa. Then, I went over to Mrs. Goyen. He blocked my view of her, but he seemed to be recounting his conversation, making some of the same gestures.

Mrs. Goyen got up. She wavered on her legs, and Michael immediately reached out to assist her. He lowered her back into the chair and left the room. Mrs. Goyen's eyes followed him.

Michael returned, wheeling in a wheelchair, just as I was about to tap on the glass to let Mrs. Goyen know I was outside. He helped Mrs. Goyen into the chair. And wheeled her toward the entry.

Mrs. Goyen didn't look frightened or as if she was being held against her will. But why were they here? Did she think she could move back to the house where she'd once been happy, and this young man would take care of her? Immediately, Mrs. Goyen's conversation in the office at Oaks came back to me: *They aren't getting another cent of Bernie's money.* And she'd given the caller Michael's name. Had he manipulated her with affection to change her will to leave her estate to him?

There was no reason to call the police as far as I could see. Mrs. Goyen didn't look like she was being held against her will. If Michael coerced her to include him in her estate, that wasn't illegal. Just criminal.

There was only one thing to do. I had to get Mrs. Goyen back to Oaks Manor.

CHAPTER THIRTY-SEVEN

The neighbor's dog began barking. Crouching to lessen my physical appearance but still allowing me to creep around the house. I found no unlocked windows. And most were too high for me to climb into without a ladder. A window in the back, blinds closed, showed a shadow of light. But, if Mrs. Goyen and Michael had come to this room, it was well insulated. I heard no voices. The only door to the house was the backdoor—locked. How could I get inside, without Michael hearing me, get Mrs. Goyen out to my car and back to Oaks?

Back at the front porch, I peeked again through the front room window. Neither of the two was in sight. What to do?

At the front door, I considered just knocking. Ask for Mrs. Goyen, saying that I was a neighbor and saw she'd returned. Then, I could get Mrs. Goyen to come with me. But if Michael attacked me, how could I stop him? And just as I redecided to call the police, I reached out and tried the door. Unlocked.

The door opened without a squeak. I traveled the same way I'd seen Michael take Mrs. Goyen and found a small hall from the back of the living room, which took me to the room with the blinds at the back of the house. The door was open. Michael was bent over. A syringe in hand.

I ran. Leaped on him. Both of us tumbled to the floor.

"Let him go," Mrs. Goyen shouted.

I was sitting on top of him, but not for long. He pushed me off, then grabbed me up, and tossed me in a chair. " Not recognizing me from my visit at Oaks, he demanded, who the hell are you?"

"The town's busybody." Mrs. Goyen shouted.

Very insulting since she was the one who had praised my busybodiness when she wanted to use me.

"I've called the police," I told him. "I gave them your name."

Having come loose from my tackle, he brushed his hair back from his face.

"Michael, my leg is cramping." Mrs. Goyen cried.

"Stay right there," Michael directed. "She needs her shot."

"Don't you do anything until the police get here." Of course, I hadn't called the police, but my confusion about what was playing out hadn't been sorted.

"He found the syringe. Went over to a stand where I saw an assortment of bottles and prescriptions. He took a cotton ball, soaked it in what smelled like alcohol, wiped the syringe, tested it by pumping out a small amount, and then went over to where Mrs. Goyen was struggling to reach down to her leg.

She was dressed in the same small satin-type gown. Her long white hair hid her face. But both hands grasped, trying to take hold of her thigh as if by her strength alone she could wring out the pain.

Michael went to her. With gentle ease, he pulled her back down, her face drained as pale as her gown, her cheeks sunken, and her eyes bulging.

"Here, you'll feel better in a minute." He raised her covers, gently pushed her onto her side while lifting her gown, and gave her the shot. Recovered her.

She lay with her eyes closed. And slowly, the muscles in her face relaxed. But, the grasping of one hand remained.

Mrs. Goyen had been compliant. No protest. Was it because of her need for her medication? Or because she wasn't opposed to Michael being in her house. He possibly wasn't keeping her without her protest, but I'd read about Stockholm Syndrome, whereby the person held developed positive feelings for those who held them. Mrs. Goyen had become fond of him.

Michael's back was to me. I glanced around, looking for something I could use as a weapon.

He held out his hand. "Micheal Day. And you are?"

"Don't you mean Micheal Goyen?" I accused.

He shot me a quick, curious look. "That's right. I use the name Day professionally."

I raised my voice so Mrs. Goyen could hear me clearly. " Michael is not a licensed nurse. And he didn't come to Oaks Manor to volunteer. He's..."

"My husband's grandson."

Shocked, I half raised off the chair. "You know?"

"Well, of course, I knew," Mrs. Goyen snapped. "He is the spitting image of his grandfather."

And she was right. Now that I took him in, he had the same eyebrows. A mustache instead of a goatee but a pointed chin. And, with his hair back behind his ears, they stood out away from his head slightly.

I sat back. More confused. "But when did you know? Before or after I went to Pella?"

"Michael," help me. He returned to her, helping her to sit up. "Do you want to get up?"

"Not yet, dear. I have no strength." She said to me. "I needed you to verify some things before I approached Michael."

Michael took up the story for her. "I think Aurelia knew who I was soon after I started coming to Oaks Manor." He smiled. "I know I take after my grandfather, but I didn't think she would make me immediately."

"Looks just like what Bernie did at his age. At first, I thought I was hallucinating." She giggled. "I felt twenty all over again."

I challenged him. "Why are you doing this? Are you after vengeance for your grandfather's bigotry? I know you've talked Mrs. Goyen into changing her will."

"He's done no such thing," Mrs. Goyen barked. "No one talks me into doing anything I don't want to do. And how do you know my business?"

"I am a busybody," I snapped. "What you called investigator when you wanted me involved in all this."

Michael was ping-ponging. He held up a hand. "I assure you, I know nothing about Aurelia changing her will." He said to her, "And I have no want of your money." To me, he explained, "I just wanted to meet her. My grandfather was not a bad man. And I wouldn't say he was deceitful. My Grandmother Day knew he was married. But, he was not a bigamist. His grandfather gave my father his name at birth. And my grandmother had gone by his last name as a way to protect my father. But, they weren't legally married."

"Well, of course not. What stupid person would think they were?"

Thinking raising my hand wasn't required, I said, "Then, none of this bothers you? You just wanted to meet Mrs. Goyen?"

Michael sat on the bed beside her. He took her grasping hand into his, caressing it until it calmed and her fingers wrapped around his.

"My generation is different than yours. The secret's out. Our parents are not perfect. Books, movies, and music have become hits because the lyrics spoke of feelings people didn't want to admit. That life is not perfect. Shit happens. Dylan, in *You're Gonna Make Me Lonely* When You Go, speaks on marriage failing and having an affair."

"I tried to make him happy," Mrs. Goyen said quietly. "But I was so sick when I first came down with this dreadful disease. Doctors kept saying they couldn't tell me how long I might live. Or how badly I'd be incapacitated."

"This is for all the lonely people who think life has passed them by," Michael sang. He caressed her cheek. "Both of you had to have been very lonely. And I think my Grandmother was also lonely. She told me she never found anyone she thought she could trust to give her life to. Until she met my grandfather."

Mrs. Goyen nodded. Her eyes warmed, returning the love she had for this young man. "His affair really wasn't a surprise. He was away too often on business. More than he'd ever traveled." She paused, her eyes saddened. "But, he always came back to me. And I couldn't give him a real life anymore. Not a life a man needs." She said, "I wish I would have told him I knew. I should have told him that it was all right. If he wanted to leave me," she hesitated. Whispered, "Get a divorce, I wouldn't like it, but I would have understood."

The room became quiet. Then Michael said, "There's no rewinding the clock. And my Grandmother says she always knew. He never lied to her. And she loved him. And when she became pregnant, he wanted to make it right somehow. He was there for the birth. He gave my father his name. And, while my father never knew his parents weren't married, they, like many, tried to keep their relationship situation concealed for his sake. Secrets never stay secret. When my grandfather died, my father confronted my Grandmother about what he'd always suspected." He said, "Children always put the truth together, but they become as good as their parents at swallowing it down."

"Was I angry?" He asked. "Furious. At all of them. I felt like my whole life was a lie. But, when I learned of Aurelia's illness, I could understand. And then, I decided I needed to understand why my Grandfather decided to live two lives inside of one. So, I came to meet Aurelia. And, when I got to know her, I understood."

I was trying to take all of this in. And, I had trouble accepting his affection toward Mrs. Goyen. She came across to me as a bitter, controlling woman. But, watching, there was no doubt she was different when she was with him.

I tendered, "Nelly's worried about you." Then, I said to Michael, "I should take her back."

"Back," Mrs. Goyen shouted. "I'm not going anywhere. I'm back home where I belong." She informed me, "I have hired Michael. He will get the house when I die, and what money is left in the estate. He can continue his musical career living here."

"But..."

"No buts. He's learned how to take care of me. And with these new medications, I am much better. Or as good as I can be at this age. Who thought I'd live this long? Not me. And I bet Bernie didn't think I would, either. I can get around a bit on my own now."

"For now," Michael said to her. "Now is all we can count on. If you get worse, you must return to Oaks Manor."

I could tell that Mrs. Goyen wasn't happy hearing this truth. But, in her mind, she was back at the beginning, not the end. She said, her eyes adoring Micheal standing beside her. "Some expectations do come true."

Micheal smiled lovingly at her, then said to me, "We've decided that during the week, she'll stay at Oaks, where she can get the assistance I can't give her. On weekends, I'll bring her here. So she'll have the best of both." Again, he caressed her cheek. "And if the time comes when the weekends need to stop, then they do. But I will still be here."

CHAPTER THIRTY-EIGHT

O f course, the police weren't going to arrive because I had never called them. And Michael must have sensed this. Because when I left, he said he would have Mrs. Goyen call Nelly and make her aware she wouldn't be back until Monday. Then, he asked if he could have them call me if they needed further explanation.

Diving home, I tried to put together all that I had learned. It wasn't lost on me how the Goyen's situation paralleled Charles' marriage. Only, maybe Michael was right, times had changed in how people were handling the skeletons in the cupboard. Cupboard doors were being thrown open. Charles's wife knew about his dating. I'd met his daughter. But did I want to live my life as the woman in-between? I told him it was over. And I think I still felt that way.

The lights were on in the house. Dahlia was up. I thought she might understand the Goyen story. Her life hadn't gone as she had planned either. She had lived secrets. And while I didn't think she had had affairs, she was far too busy surviving with a husband drinking his life away and rebellious children trying to exist in a world of puzzling riddles. *Why me? Why is my family not like everyone else's?* Back when raising us, the concept of protecting children came from the thought that what they don't know won't hurt them.

Just as I was about to go inside. When something was placed over my nose and mouth. A sweet, flowery, alcoholic....

I awoke with a start. My head pounded. My mouth was dry as if it was stuffed with cotton. I was lying on a wooden floor, slumped against a wall. My arms felt wrung as if stretched to their limit. My ribs ached as I tried to straighten up. My wrists and ankles were bound. Panic rose in my chest as I realized what had happened. I had been kidnapped.

"Are you okay?"

My head jerked around. I didn't know I wasn't alone. Across from me sat a young woman, her hair styled in a bob. Nola.

"No," I moaned.

I glanced around. The small room was dimly lit, and we were alone. Our captor was nowhere to be seen. Fear and dread coursed through me. I squirmed, testing the strength of the bindings. Then, instinctively, I opened my mouth as if to scream for help.

"Don't," the young woman warned me. "He hates it when you scream."

Then I noticed the dark purple bruise under her eye—a red stain across her cheek.

"Did Randall Caruthers do this?"

She shook her head.

"Then his dad?"

"I don't know the man's name, okay?" She almost sounded angry at my wrong guessing. "Janice and I were down at the lake, and this guy came out of nowhere. I mean, it was like he flew out of nowhere. He knocked me to the ground. I think my head hit something because I blacked out. And when I woke up, I saw him attacking Janice. And. I started screaming." Her voice choked. Tears began dripping off her quivering chin. "I think he'd forgotten all about me. Then he started dragging Janice into the lake. But she continued to fight him. And she almost got away, but then..." her words stopped. Her lips trembled with the memory. She gagged and gasped, "He killed her. And then I heard voices. And I started screaming for help. I knew he was going to kill me, too. But he didn't. He put something over my mouth, and next I know, I'm here."

I tried to digest what she was telling me. "Do you know where here is?"

She shook her head. "Nowhere good."

I tried again to get free, but it only made what was binding me dig deeper into my flesh.

I was suddenly freezing as if I'd just stepped into a freezer. My chin trembled uncontrollably at my realization that I might be helplessly trapped. Choices limited—future unknown. And the possibility of being rescued was hopeless. Dahlia would eventually wonder why I hadn't returned. She'd be waiting to hear what had happened to Mrs. Goyen. And if she called Nelly again, she'd learn part of the story. Checking outside, she'd find my car. Maybe she'd even heard me drive in. But, I sincerely doubted she heard me taken. I hadn't heard someone step behind me. And I was out before I could scream.

Leveque? He was after the wrong person. And, I might have been the one who led him in the wrong direction if he knew about my meeting Randall.

I asked, trying to piece together how I could have been so wrong. "What were you and Janice doing at the lake?"

"It was all Randall's idea," she said. "He had me pretend to be kidnapped and told me to say I was in a basement so the police would think I was at his Dad's." She added, "The police thought his dad was the August Lake killer, but they couldn't prove it. So Randall wanted to do what the police couldn't."

"Where were you when you called me?" And I had to add, "I was the one who answered your 911 call."

She seemed surprised at how small her world had become. "I was at home."

"But I heard a man's voice," I told her.

"It was Randall. He was with me when I called. At first, I didn't want to do it, but he said it was time to show his old man he couldn't get away with killing his mother. He's so sure his dad is the August Lake killer. And he said this time, he wasn't going to let his dad get away with it. But when he left after I called, I got scared. I was worried that I'd be arrested for lying to the police. My parents would be furious. They hated that Randall and I were still friends. They said they couldn't wait for me to go back to school and how it might be better to stay at the college if I was going to see the likes of him."

She choked back a sob. Tears streamed down her face.

While all that made sense, I still couldn't put together how she ended up here."

"But I still don't understand why you were at the lake."

"That was Janice's idea. She said the cop that questioned her kept implying Randall was lying about where he was and seemed like he thought Randall might have drowned the girl they found. Like he was taking after his dad or something. So, Janice thought we could plant something of his dad's down at the lake. Randall gave her the hat his Dad wore. We were going to hide it in the bushes. Only when we were trying to decide where might be a good place, this man jumped us. And..."

My heart was racing, and my breathing came in shallow breaths as my fate became clear. Randall wanting me to tell the police his father was the killer made sense now. He hadn't known Janice had been killed. Leveque was following the wrong clues. Just as I had been putting the pieces together wrongly. And if Dahlia called the police, they wouldn't have any idea where to start searching for me. Did anyone know Nola was missing? Would they put the disappearance of the two of us together?

"Now lookie what we have here."

Otis Gusta came into the room so stealthily I didn't discern a shift in movement. But I caught the odor of ammonia before seeing him. He approached Nola, offering her a bottle of water which she drank with enthusiasm. But, when he turned to me, I averted my gaze.

"Better get hydrated. It'll be a while until we get where we're going. And there'll be no stops along the way."

"They'll be looking for us," I warned.

"No doubt. Two fine girls like you. But they don't know about me. I've been too smart for them. Damn fools couldn't catch me the last time I was here. And they're falling over their feet now."

"I have to go to the bathroom," Nola interrupted.

He turned to her and grinned. "Well, now. Let's see what we can do about that." He went over. Pulled a small pocket knife out of this pocket. Nola gasped at seeing it. She started to wiggle away from him. He leaned down and cut the restraints at her ankles. "Here, let me help you up. I won't be able to release your hands, but I'd be happy to assist you with your clothing."

The mere thought of him touching her broke Nola. Tears streamed down her face as she silently sobbed. I could tell she wanted to say something, but her emotion had taken her voice away.

Her eyes turned to me. I shook my head, silently warning her not to provoke him.

He lowered himself and retied her. "Suit yourself. But I bet we'll become good friends sooner than later. If you know what's good for you." He stood. "We leave in a few minutes, ladies."

"What are we going to do?" Nola whispered when he'd left.

"I don't know." My eyes darted around the room, my heart racing as I scanned for anything to protect myself. When he helped me to my feet to walk out of there, I knew it might be the only time I'd have an opportunity to get away. I had no idea where he was going to take us. Maquoketa? And what did he plan to do with us? I stopped my mind from racing beyond where we were now.

But I found nothing in the room to help. No rugs on the floor. A small table over in the corner with a chair. I could see a plate and cutlery. If I could get close enough to grab the fork, I may be able to use it as a weapon. I told Nola, "He has to untie us so we can walk out of here. I'll try to trip him or do something to take his notice. Then, when I do, run. Don't look back. Run like your life depends on it."

"But what about you? He'll kill you."

"I have a feeling that's in our future anyway. So we might as well make it hard for him."

We were quiet. Fear silencing us. Nola, like me, may have been thinking of those we'd be leaving behind and not having the chance to say goodbye. Or to tell them we loved them. Nola's parents were probably already worried sick. And Dahlia? My mother wouldn't be satisfied until she learned what had happened to me and the person responsible. I knew my mother. She could be ruthless and wouldn't leave the police alone until she had answers.

I guess we were a little alike. But, of course, that wasn't a bad thing at this point.

This time when Gusta came back into the room, we both turned. He was wearing a coat and carrying a couple of blankets. He went over to Nola first. "Okay, darlin', let's get going." He pulled out his pocket knife again and cut her ankles loose. Again, she instinctually drew away as he moved to take her arm, but his sense of levity was gone. He grabbed her. Pulled her up sharply. She cried out in pain. Stood unsteady, her legs weak from having been sitting on the floor for so long.

"Let me go," she demanded. He drew back his hand and slapped her across the face. "We're going to do this nice and quiet like. Aren't we?"

She started crying uncontrollably, but when he raised his hand again, she stopped. She peeked over at me. I tried to smile. I wanted to give her hope. I gave my head a backward jerk, motioning for her to try to get him close to me. But as he took her to the doorway, he made a wide circle around, keeping both of them far from any attempt I could make.

He opened the door. Gave a look outside. "Come on. And not a word." He showed her his knife, reminding her what would happen if she didn't do as he asked.

They had barely stepped out when I heard, "Let her go and put your hands up.

No denying whose voice it was. Charles.

And then, to my relief, I saw Sargarent Miner's face. He'd come around the back. He put a finger to his lips and hurried over to me.

"Stay back," Gusta yelled, "or she's dead."

Miner started releasing me, whispering, "Stay quiet. I'll get you out of here."

But once untied, I refused to get up and go with him. "We need to do something."

He pulled out his revolver and went over to the doorway. Checked the situation. Stay down. I'll get you safe first."

I thought quickly. Said, "He didn't hear you. He'll think I'm still tied up. If I run out, it'll surprise him. And it might just give you time to get Nola away from him. Give Charles the chance to take control."

"Too dangerous. You could get shot. Now come on." He walked back to me.

"Let her go, Gusta," another voice shouted. This time it was Leveque's. We know who you are. And what you've done."

"Then, killing this here girl will be on you, not me."

"Let me go," Nola screamed.

And I hoped she was struggling against his holding her. Trying to get away from him before he did kill her just to prove his point to the police.

I ran out the door. "Run, Nola! Run!?

Otis Gusta jerked around at hearing my voice. He was just off balance enough that when Nola pushed against him, she freed herself. And ran.

"Put your hands up. Get on the ground." Leveque ordered.

"Throw down your weapon," Sergeant Miner demanded.

Sergeant Miner's voice coming from behind him took Gusta by surprise. "On the ground."

He turned from one command to the next. And then spotted me again. I had stopped running when Nola got away, thinking the situation was handled.

Gusta flew toward me. Like he'd taken flight, his feet left the ground. His weight hit me. I felt the sharp edge of the blade.

And a rally of shots rang out.

"Get off me!" I screamed, wanting his vile body off me.

A metallic odor began smothering the scent of ammonia reeking from his coat. His grizzled beard scratched my face. His eyes-- lifeless.

"Lillian?"

Gusta's body was rolled off me

Leveque half lifted me off the ground. "What the hell are you doing here?" But his voice wasn't accusatory. Instead, his words came softly against me as his arms circled me. "I could have shot you."

"I pulled partly back." Smiled. "In your dreams."

And I saw Charles. And Garth Davis. And others coming out from where they were hidden. Finally, Charles came over to us. "You okay, Lil?"

"Maybe not okay, but I am a whole lot better than I thought I'd be."

CHAPTER THIRTY-NINE

The crime scene became active. The ambulance arrived, and EMTs checked on Nola and me. They wanted to take us to the hospital, but we both refused. Nola just wanted to go home. And Charles told Officer Garth Davis to take her. Crime scene tape was being strung up. A forensic team arrived. Leveque came over and handed me a phone.

Charles said, "Donna has told your mother you're all right, but I think you'd better call her. She's pretty insistent on talking to you."

I walked away from the activity and dialed home. Dahlia answered on the first ring. "Who is this?" she demanded. No hello. She wasn't in the mood for trivial greetings.

"It's me," I said.

I heard an enormous sigh of relief. "Are you all right?"

"Yes."

Another sigh. "Bacardi and I will wait for you to get home."

Not Bud. And my heart overflowed.

Charles came over. "I'll take you to the station."

I nodded. Looked back to the house where Otis Gusta had kept us captive. A nondescript house with a neglected yard and a For Rent sign.

On the way to the station, I asked. "How is your wife?"

"She's going to be okay."

"I'm glad."

"We'll talk about that later. Right now, my concern is for you. Are you okay?"

"I am."

And I was.

But it wasn't until I was back home with Dahlia and Bacardi that I felt safe. When Officer Garth dropped me home, she enveloped me in a warm hug. I told her everything that had happened. She listened, her face a mask covering what fear and worry she'd felt, instead offering me sympathy and understanding. She hushed me when I tried to tell her more, and she said, "No more tonight. You need a hot shower. And sleep."

I stripped off my clothes, still with a slight ammonia scent from Gusta's lying on top of me. I stepped into the hot spray. Letting the warm water ease me, loosen my tenseness, and clean me from what had happened. A light tap came at the door. Dahlia came in, setting clean pajamas on the sink. Bacardi curled in around her before she closed the door. He sat down, his smashed face scrunched even tighter as he glared at me. As is saying, "What did you do this time?"

And then I cried. Letting the hot spray pull the fear out of me. Allowing the tears to flow freely, wanting to let it all out. I didn't want to give Gusta's evil any power over me. While I'd never forget what happened or forget him, I would not let him plague my nightmares.

Out of the shower, Dahlia brought me one of my favorite teas, *Sleepytime*. Then, she hushed me, "We'll talk more tomorrow. You need to get some rest."

I crawled into the covers. Bacardi jumped up and nested in at the bottom of the bed. But I couldn't sleep.

My mind went over everything. How I'd confused the past with the present. The researched articles on DeWade as a past subject. And Leveque's determination to catch him this time. Revenging mistakes he thought he'd made. I saw then how what goes on Google, recording history, both true and untrue, can create impressions. If no one heard about Gusta being arrested and read how he was the August Lake killer, they would continue thinking DeWade Carruthers had got away with murder.

And then, a name came into my mind. Helen Morales. Leveque had mentioned her in his drunken call raging at me that I was ruining his case. But who was she? Was she still missing? And who was the woman in my dreams who begged me to help them? Was she the girl still missing from the murders six years ago?

I got up. It was late. Bacardi jumped off the bed as I dressed. He followed me out to the front door. "Stay here. I'm done with getting in trouble."

I got into the Mustang and headed across town.

CHAPTER FORTY

He immediately opened the door as if he, too, hadn't been able to sleep. As if he had been waiting for me.

"Helen Morales?"

"Later." He pulled me inside, taking me into his arms. My fingers pulled to his bare skin as his lips kissed my ears and neck. His hands moved through my hair, bringing me closer as if not wanting any space between us.

When we parted, he smiled. "I must be dreaming. "

"Don't wake up," I laughed. I moved to him and kissed him. A kiss letting him know it was all right. That for tonight, I wanted him as much as he wanted me. In this moment, maybe just this moment.

He pulled off my T-shirt. Threw off my bra. And tenderly he cupped my breasts, and then with an excel of breath, his hands moved down to my waist, fingers creeping under the waistband. He unzipped my jeans, and his fingers found what they sought. Until we both had no breath left. Panting. Wanting.

Taking my hand, he led me through the house. And I followed. At his bedroom door, his mouth took mine, hungry. My hands moved through his curls, encouraging. In a breathless rush, we went to bed. I fell in without words. His body was powerful. His touch was gentle. His lips explored every inch of my body. And his inches not holding back until if he hadn't entered me, I would have tossed him over and taken him. I wanted him.

No more thinking. No more rationalizing how this could be a big mistake. I wanted him more than I had ever wanted a man.

We explored and pleasured each other until the sun came up. And with the first signs of another day, I wasn't sure I was the same Lillian I had been before. Or if I would be her again. Experiences change us. Events make up who we are. And I knew I had opened my heart to him like I hadn't opened it to anyone else. And, somehow, I knew he had given me more than he had ever expected.

He got up and brought back water. We drank the water eagerly as if we had been lost in a desert. Our smiles came at the same time. "Surprise!" He joked.

I wrapped the sheet around me. I emptied the bottle before saying, "Yes. But a nice surprise."

We then went over what had happened. He repeated what I learned at the station. That Gusta had dropped one of his gloves. Bat guano was found embedded in it. And Officer Davis remembered pulling over an old guy in a truth that talked his ear off about bats. They had been zeroing in on Gusta as a possible suspect. Leveque's new lead. When Janice was killed, and Nola went missing, the investigation intensified.. Gusta's truck was spotted and followed.

"We did not know you were involved until you came out of that house." He drew me to him. "But, I should have known." And he kissed me. This time slow, patient, willing to hold back the hungry for what might lie beneath it.

He fell asleep. And I lay beside him. Watching him sleep. We never spoke of Helen Morales. Maybe he wanted to move past moments he couldn't relive as much as I tried to move beyond mine.

I thought then of how Mrs. Goyen initially wanted revenge against the family Bernie had made beyond her. And how she was now embracing a part of that family, accepting it in part as hers. Randall wanted vengeance because he thought his father had killed his mother. But his father repeated his story to the police that his wife left one night after an argument, and he hadn't heard from her. And my night with Leveque? Funny how *never* comes around to bite you in the butt.

Is that what living life with a vengeance means? Grabbing moments as they come? Satiating desires as I felt them?

And after? I fell asleep without that answer.

But maybe that's the answer. I didn't have to understand everything that had happened right now. There would be more moments ahead. Experiences to be had. Maybe the answers would come when it was time for me to embrace them.

CHAPTER FORTY-ONE
SATURDAY, FEBRUARY 14TH

I woke up, my eyes moving from Leveque to the bedside clock. Almost eleven. What day is it?

Leveque moaned. Opened his eyes.

My head cleared. "Shit, I've got to go."

"Not yet," Leveque reached for me.

I jumped out of bed. Grabbed my clothes. "I've got to go. I'm late opening Discount."

He sat up. "I'm late going into the station. But, I'm willing to..."

I ran to the bathroom to dress. When I came out, he was there, waiting.

"I'll call you later," he leaned over.

I pulled back. "Look, Leveque. I'm not sure what this is between us. And I am not ready for a relationship."

"Hey, if you're worried about Charles."

"I told Charles the same."

I hurried to the front door.

"I don't understand." He followed. "We both felt something last night, right?"

"I'm not a notch on your belt."

His face fell. "You think that's what last night meant to me?"

"I need to make sure what it meant to me." I didn't mean to hurt him, but I wanted to take this moment seriously. "I want to make sure you weren't just a notch on mine."

When I got to Discount, I saw the blue Toyota in the parking lot. Customer cars parked and moving in and out of the store. I went to where Dahlia stood behind the counter. "Are you all right?" She asked as I came around. She was finishing up a sale of Baileys to Roger Franklin, who liked a little sweetness in his coffee.

"I am." I said.

EPILOGUE

D ahlia didn't work at Discount every day after Valentine's Day. But she would come in when I became busy. The police in Maquoketa investigated the Gusta home and found items belonging to what they felt were more victims than just those of August Lake. The park was also closed as a crime site, having found remains in a few small caves closed off to the public.

As a caution that there might be more unknown victims in August Lake, Charles ordered an extensive search. Some remains were found and identified as Margaret Constance Carruthers. Cause of death left listed, UNKNOWN. Was she one of Gusta's first victims? Did her husband kill her? Or was she one of the rare drowning victims? Randall Carruthers may never have his answer. He left Frytown. I'm not sure whether he followed Nola up to Ames or if he left for places unknown to get away from his past and move on.

My contact with Charles became limited. His wife attempted suicide, and I knew all of his concern was now for her and his daughter. Leveque called once, but I told him I hadn't changed my mind. I didn't regret the night we'd spent together, but before I could commit myself to anyone else, I needed to commit myself to me. And I was just beginning to discover who I was.

Dahlia visited Mrs. Goyen. She spent the weekdays at Oaks Manor and the weekends with Michael. Dahlia said, "Aurelia looks better than she has in a long time."

I heard Percy took a brief vacation to Des Moines.

And my phone has been ringing. People have heard what I did for Mrs. Goyen and my involvement with Otto Gusta. They have been calling with minor questions. Dahlia said I was going to need a new T-shirt: Sherlock

I still never got back to Pella. And I wouldn't have left Frytown for a long while, no more time for vacations. But two months later, just as Spring was budding, and the warmth of summer promised to make the days longer and easier, Dahlia answered the phone one night.

The caller was my brother Frank. "The Dubuque Police called. Patrick is missing."

THE END

ACKNOWLEDGEMENTS

First, thank you for reading the fourth book of the Lillian Dove Series. I have put words on paper since I could hold a pencil to paper. But it is always more fun when others find they relate to some of the emotional and life-changing discoveries Lillian shares.

Of course, while I may be the one who sits at the computer, listening to Lillian's newest tale, others have also played a part. I want to thank Luanne, LaVerna, and Melanie for their comments on the completed story and structure. Thanks, too, to Rachelle LaPan, who puts up with my questions on police procedure. Fellow author Nancy Cole Silverman boosts my morale when the going gets rough. And when I am really in the blues, stuck in doubt, she picks up the check at lunch.

Thanks to the amazing bloggers and reviewers who boost my efforts with their praise. And to those who interact with me on social media. That type of support and kind messages is priceless.

My husband's loving support makes this possible.

My mother often said when she put her feet on the floor in the morning, "Well, you've given me another one. I might as well take it on."

Lillian continues to discover she can start her life anew.

F rytown is a real unincorporated community in Johnson County, Iowa, about 10 miles southwest of Iowa City. The town has been town as Frytown since the 19th Century. Lillian's Frytown is a mixture of several cities and towns in Iowa, as are many other locations in this novel. It is fictional. All characters in this work are fictitious. Any similarities to living persons are coincidental.

ABOUT THE AUTHOR

Dj received awards for her *Lillian Dove Mystery Series* featuring amateur sleuth Lillian Dove. In addition, she was nominated in 2021 for a Clue Award for her suspense crime thriller *Into the Storm*. And a 2021 Paranormal Award for *At the Edge of No Return*. Many of her psychological and suspense thrillers feature elements. Dj is the editor of Le Coeur de l'Artiste, an online book review magazine, and interviews authors on her website blog, L'Artiste. Recently retired from teaching writing and literature at Glendale College, she lives in Southern Los Angeles and on the Central Coast.

Dj loves hearing from readers and answers all emails.

For more information, visit her at http://www.djadamson.com/

To receive **FREE** Le Coeur de l'Artiste, a monthly review of books, go to http://www.djadamson.com/contact.html

ENJOYED LILLIAN? Don't miss one of the other books in the series:

BOOK ONE: ***ADMIT TO MAYHEM***: https://mybook.to/xdv6olP

BOOK TWO: ***SUPPOSE:*** https://mybook.to/xeC7

BOOK THREE: ***LET HER GO:*** https://mybook.to/8HUHry

www.ingramcontent.com/pod-product-compliance
Lightning Source LLC
Chambersburg PA
CBHW050729180626
46814CB00002B/673